# The Yak Pack

## Comics & Phonics

### Book 1: Short Vowels

Created by **r** rumack resources

Stories by Jennifer Makwana, B.Ed
Illustrated by Jalisa Henry

Ruth Rumack's Learning Space
720 Spadina Ave., Suite 504
Toronto, Ontario, Canada M5S 2T9
www.ruthrumack.com
www.rumackresources.com

Book and Cover Design: Kathleen Fasciano and Jalisa Henry
Executive in Charge of Production: Evan Brooker

ISBN: 978-0-9947637-9-2

# The Yak Pack Phonics Readers

## What are phonics readers?

Phonics readers contain stories that focus on a targeted sound. The stories are all decodable, meaning a child who knows the targeted sound will be able to sound out all of the main words in the story, based on the typical phonetic sounds made by the letters. This reader targets each of the five short vowel sounds, as well as a review of all the short vowels together.

## How do they help?

Decodable phonics readers allow a child to focus on reading phonetically-controlled words, that is, words that follow a phonetic pattern that the child understands. When a child learns a particular phonics sound, it is important to practice reading words with that sound, especially in the context of a fun story! *The Yak Pack Comics & Phonics* were written to appeal to beginning readers of all ages, with bold illustrations, fun characters, and a comic style that is sure to engage even the most reluctant reader.

## How do sight words fit in?

Sight words are service words that appear frequently in stories. Not many sentences can be made without the use of sight words. They include words like *of, to, for, the, they,* and *you,* to name just a few. Sight words are not usually decodable, and they must be memorized to assist in reading. The sight words in this reader are all high-frequency words that a beginning reader is likely to know. (For more practice with sight words, look for *The Yak Pack Sight Word Stories*, also available from Rumack Resources.)

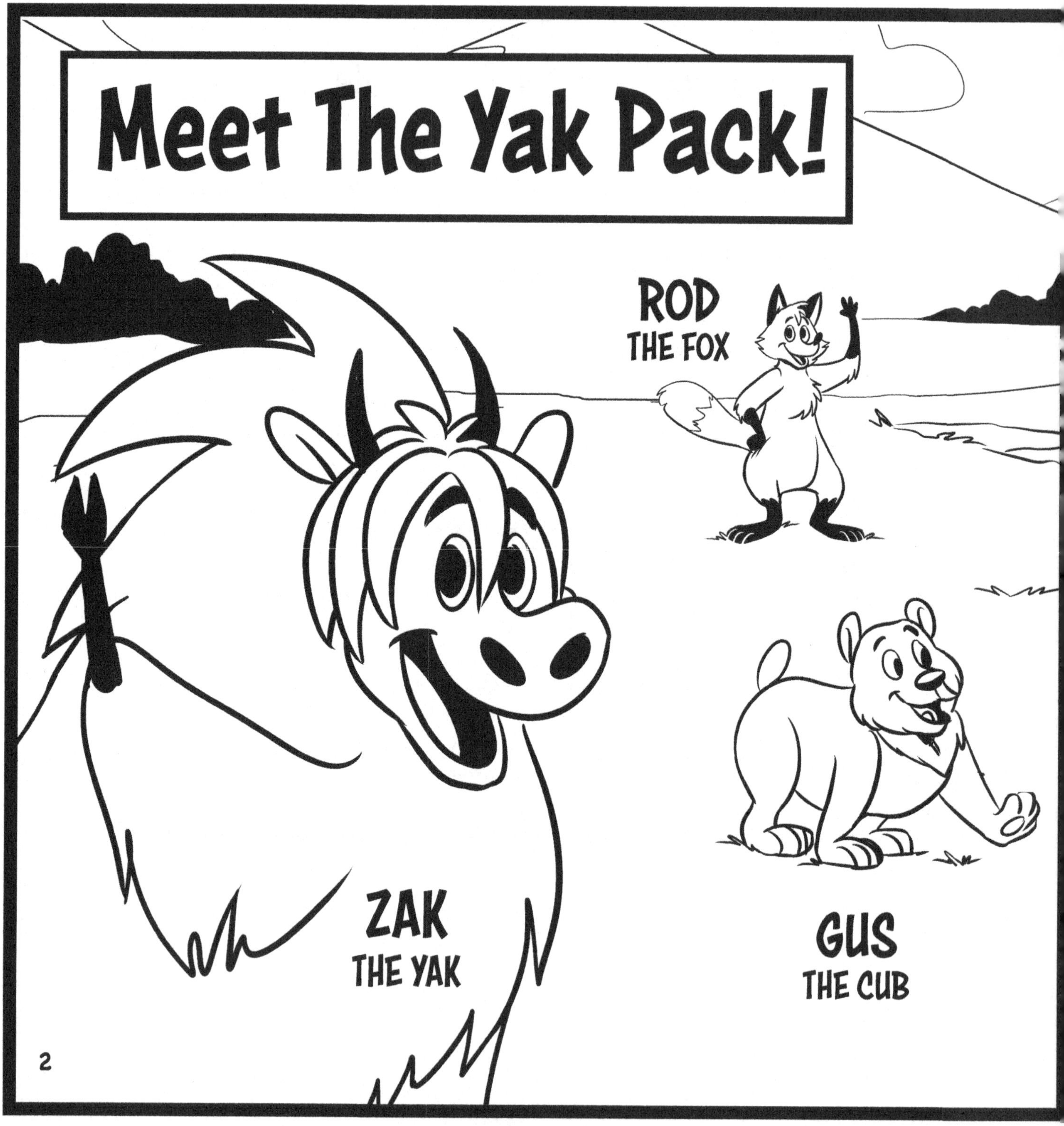
Meet The Yak Pack!
ROD
THE FOX
ZAK
THE YAK
GUS
THE CUB

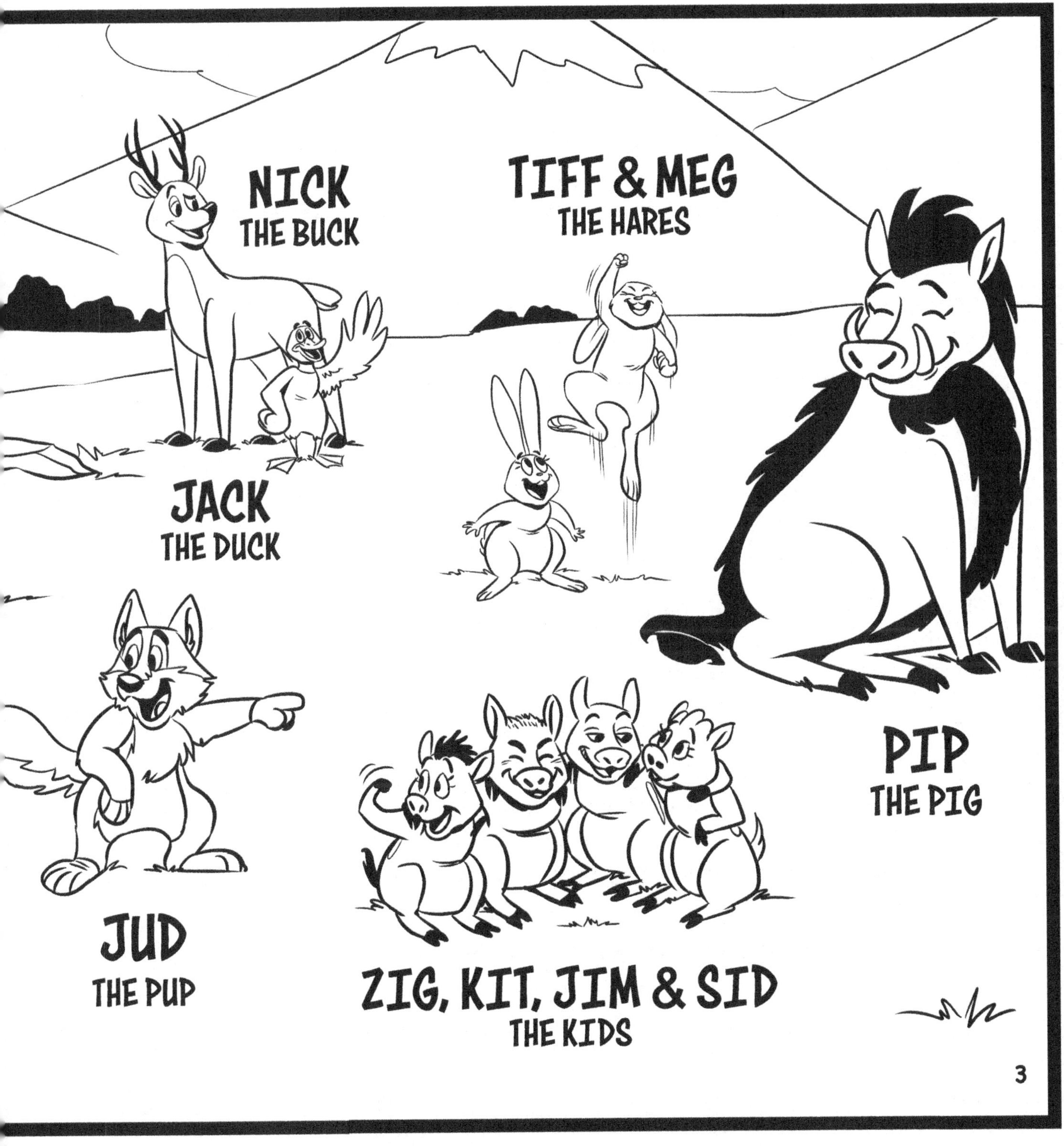
NICK
THE BUCK
TIFF & MEG
THE HARES
JACK
THE DUCK
PIP
THE PIG
JUD
THE PUP
ZIG, KIT, JIM & SID
THE KIDS

# HOW TO USE THIS BOOK

This reader is the first in *The Yak Pack Comics & Phonics* series. It contains a different comic for each short vowel sound, along with a review comic with all five vowels. For a complete list of phonics sounds covered in the series, please see page 60.

- Refer to the "In This Story" page at the beginning of each comic:
  - Ensure that your child is able to correctly pronounce the sound that is practiced.
  - Review the word list together so that your child has a chance to practice the words that will appear in the comic.
  - The sight words that will appear in the comic are listed as well. Review these with your child.
  - If noted, review any previously learned sounds.

- Have your child read the comic aloud. For beginning readers (or those new to the comic format), you may need to discuss the concept of speech bubbles and the order in which the lines should be read.

- When your child completes reading each comic, turn to the "After You Read" page that follows the story:
  - Ask your child the **comprehension questions**. Each comic contains two fact-based questions, one inference question, and one prediction question – all important skills in developing strong reading comprehension.
  - Practice the **phonological awareness skills** with your child. These include rhyming, blending, segmenting, and manipulating the sounds within words. Strong phonological awareness is an excellent predictor of reading and spelling success.

# TABLE OF CONTENTS

# STORY 1

# Zak the Yak

# SHORT A

# In This Story: Zak the Yak

| Skill Practiced: Short A | | | | | |
|---|---|---|---|---|---|
| -ak | -at | -ad | -an | -as | -ap |
| Zak | hat | tad | can | has | map |
| yak | rat | bad | ran | | |
| | fat | sad | | | |
| | | glad | | | |

| Sight Words Covered | | |
|---|---|---|
| I | have | the |
| a | put | in |
| am | to | is |

Short A makes the sound /a/, as in *apple*.

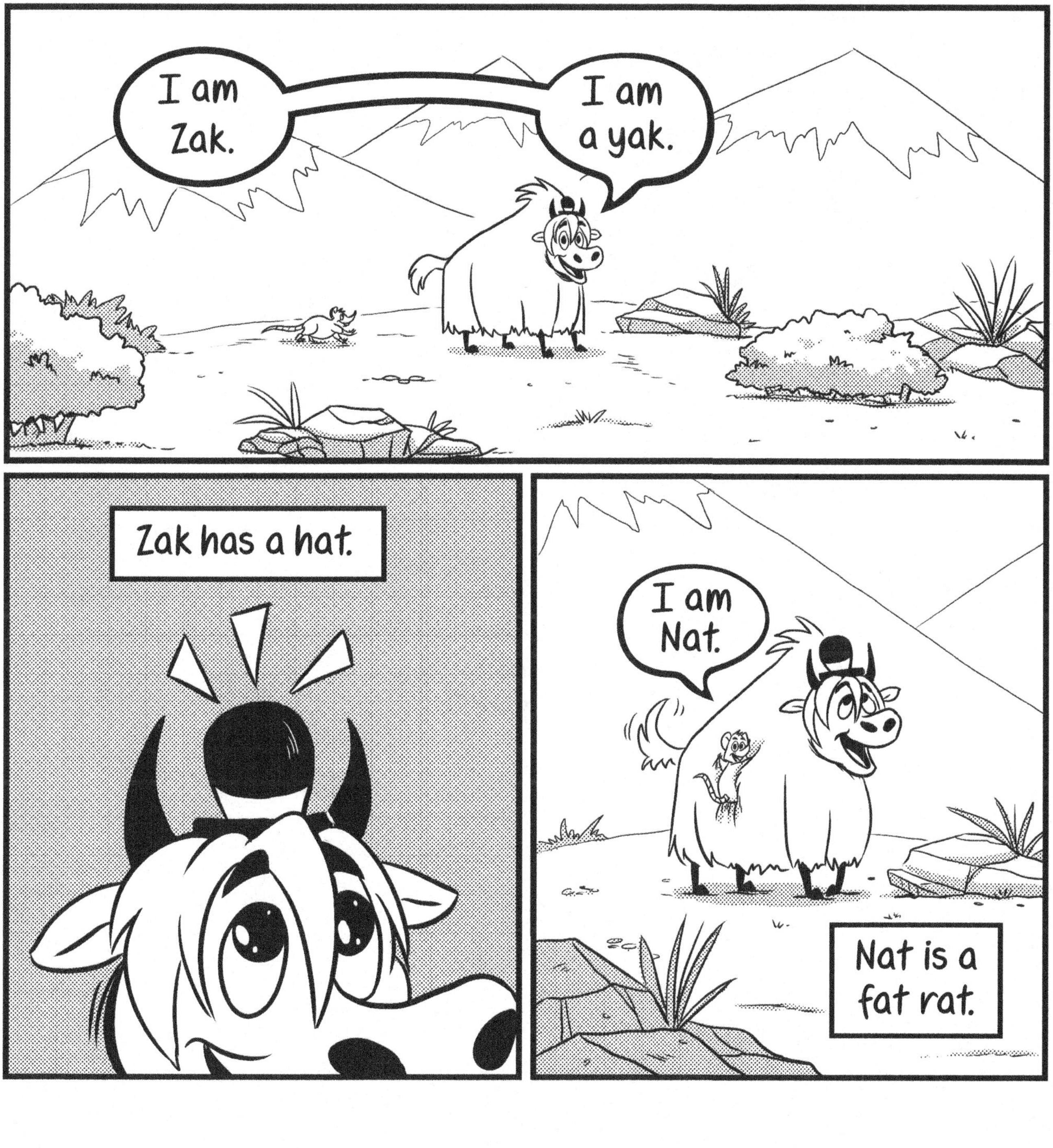
I am Zak.
I am a yak.
Zak has a hat.
I am Nat.
Nat is a fat rat.

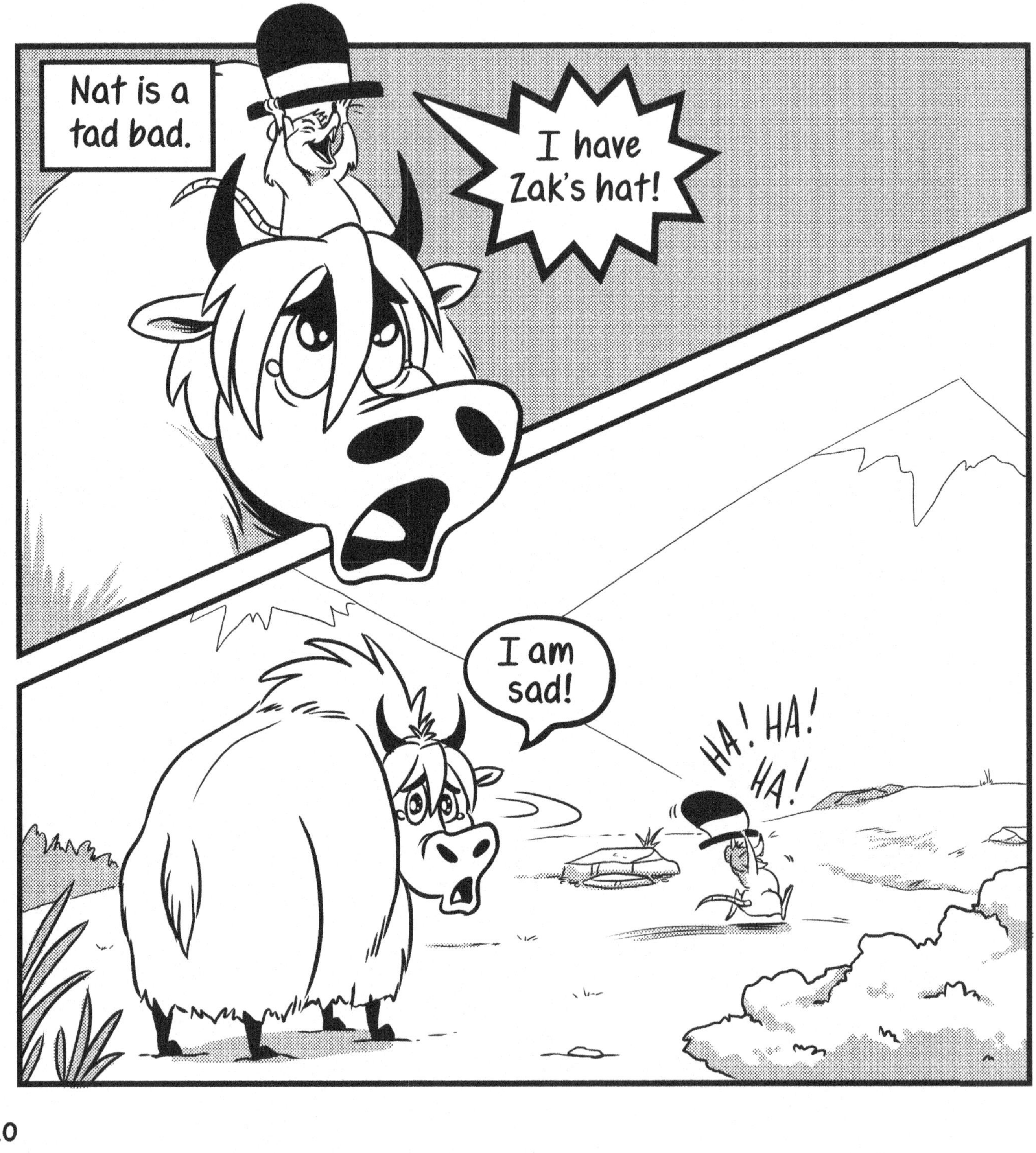
Nat is a tad bad.
I have Zak's hat!
I am sad!
HA! HA! HA!

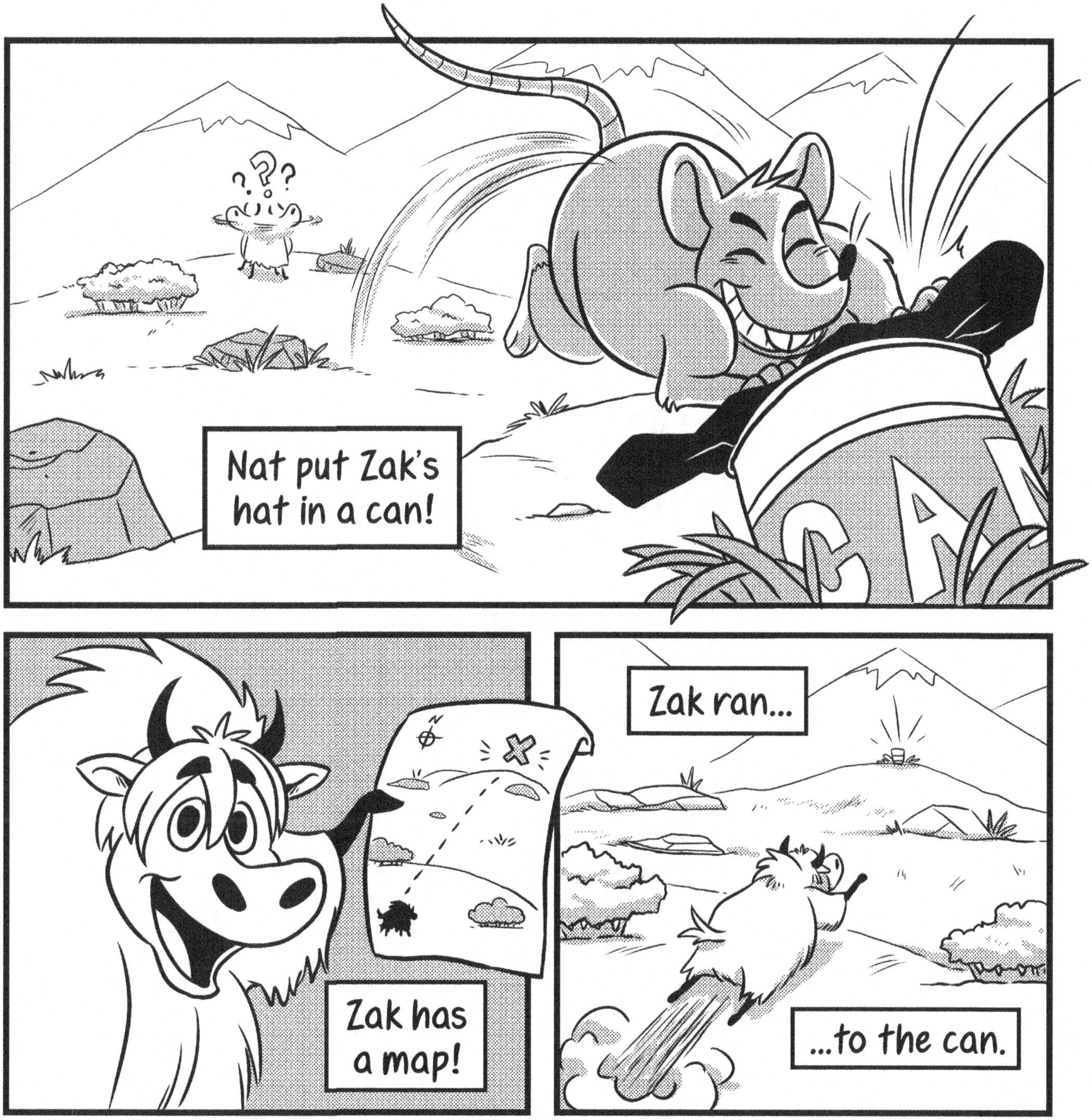
Nat put Zak's hat in a can!
CAN
Zak has a map!
Zak ran...
...to the can.

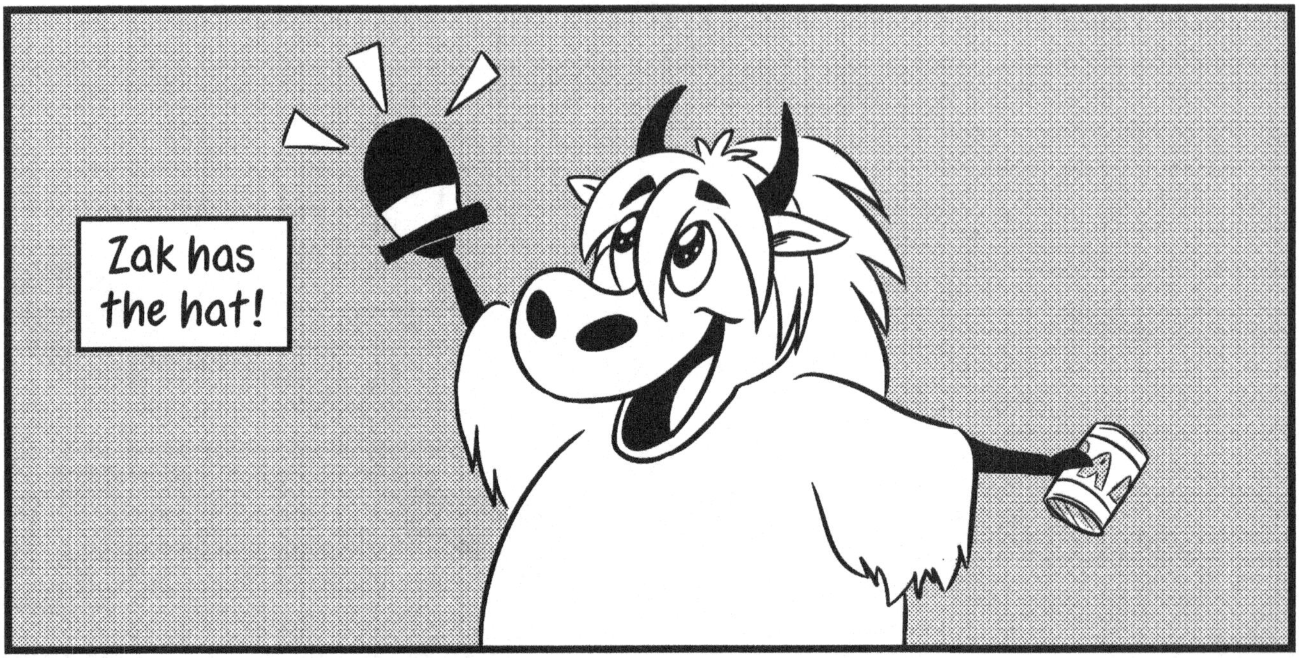
Zak has the hat!

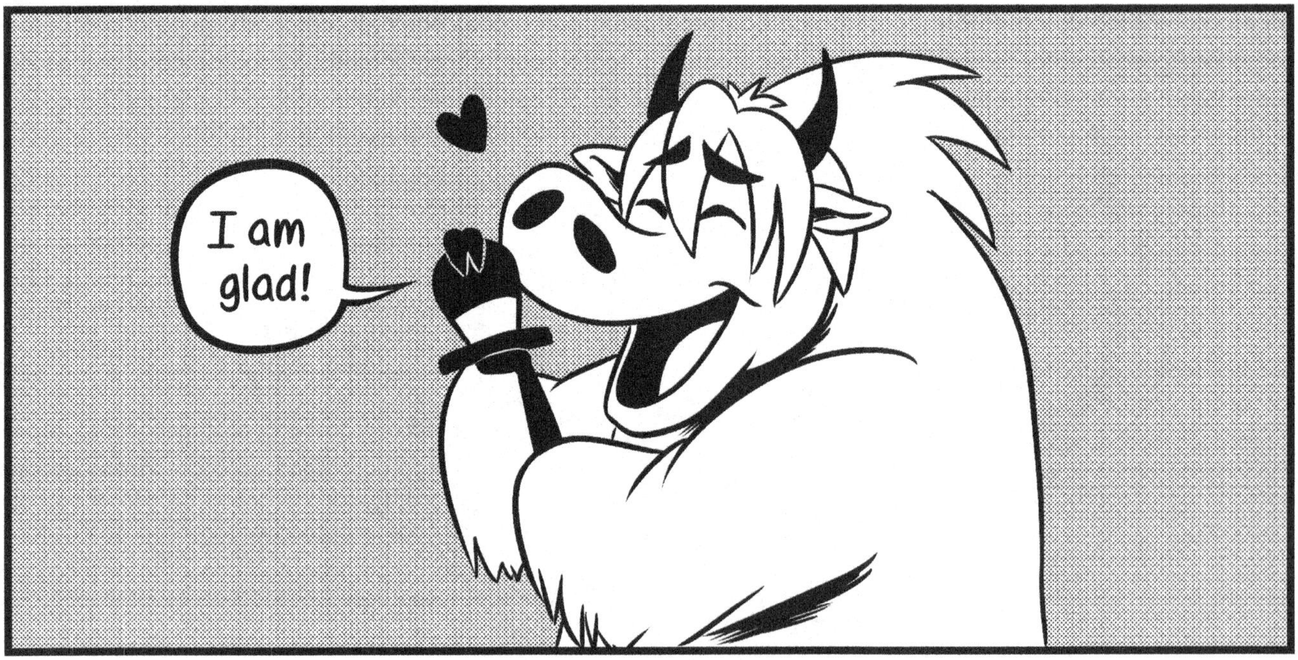
I am glad!

# After You Read: Zak the Yak

## CHECK FOR UNDERSTANDING

1. Where did Nat put Zak's hat?
2. How did Zak find his hat?
3. Why did Nat put Zak's hat in the can?
4. What other trouble do you think Nat the rat will get up to?

## PHONOLOGICAL AWARENESS SKILLS

1. What is a word that rhymes with "ran"?
2. What do you get if you blend the sounds /c/ /a/ /t/?
3. How many sounds do you hear in the word "map"?
4. Can you change the first sound in "bad" to /s/? What's the new word?

# STORY 2

# Rod Has a Job

# SHORT O

# In This Story: Rod Has a Job

| Skill Practiced: Short O | | | | | |
|---|---|---|---|---|---|
| -ox | -og | -op | -ot | -od | -ob |
| box | jog | mop | hot | Rod | job |
| fox | bog | top | cot | | |
| | log | | lot | | |
| | fog | | got | | |

| Sight Words Covered | | |
|---|---|---|
| I | he | the |
| a | in | has |
| is | to | am |
| on | at | |

Short O makes the sound /o/, as in *octopus*.

## Skills Learned Previously: Short A

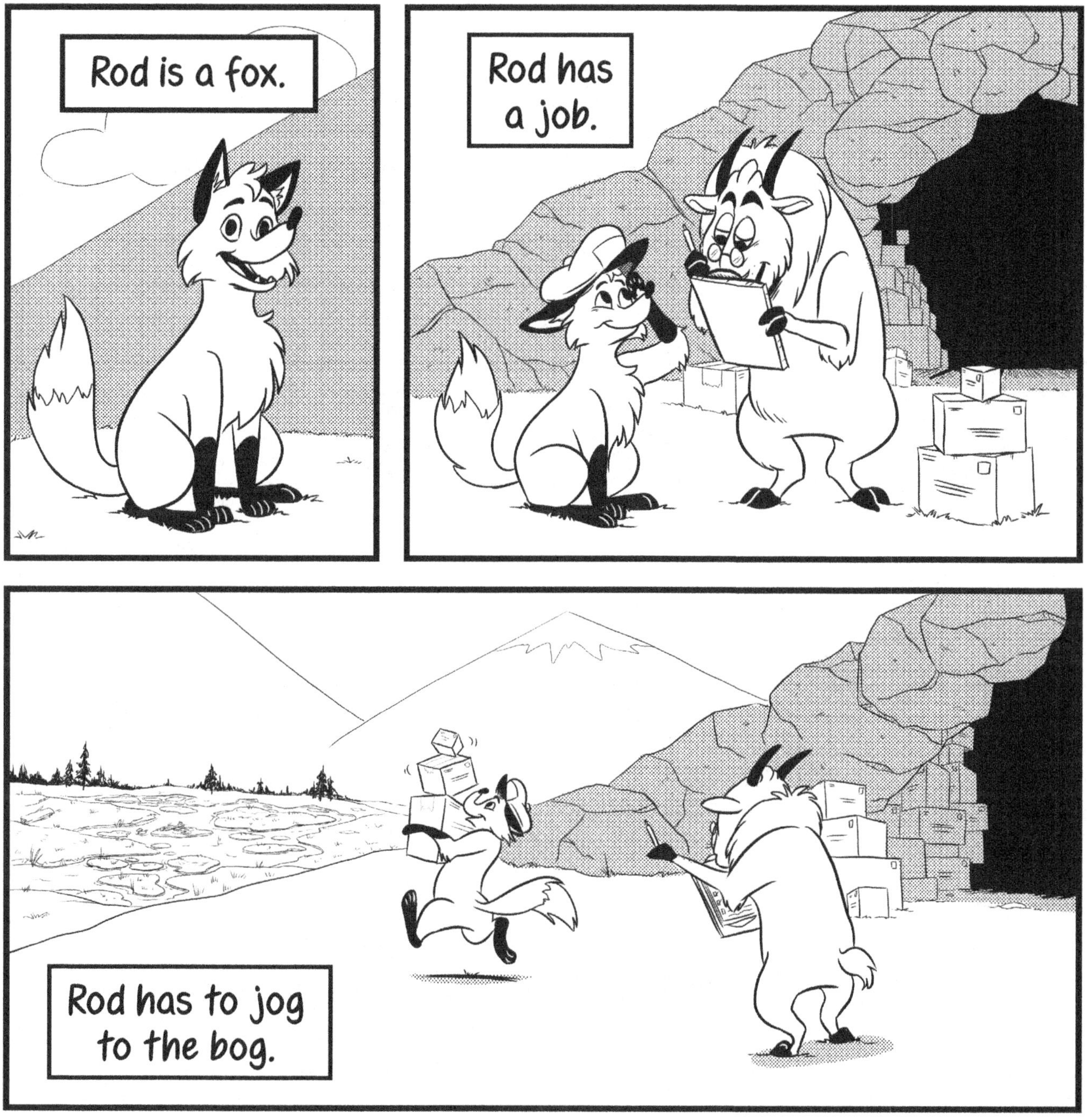
Rod is a fox.
Rod has a job.
Rod has to jog to the bog.

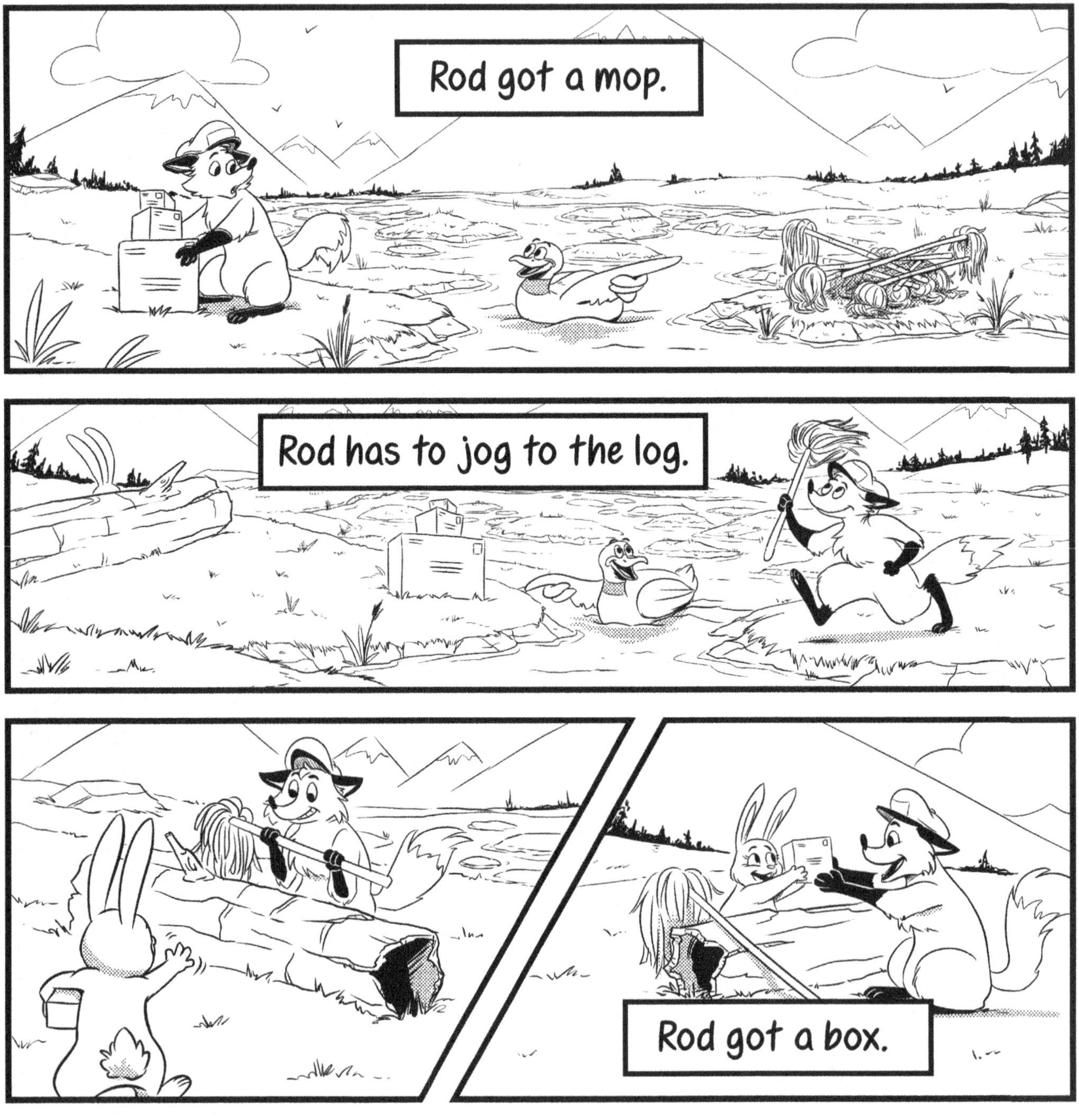
Rod got a mop.
Rod has to jog to the log.
Rod got a box.

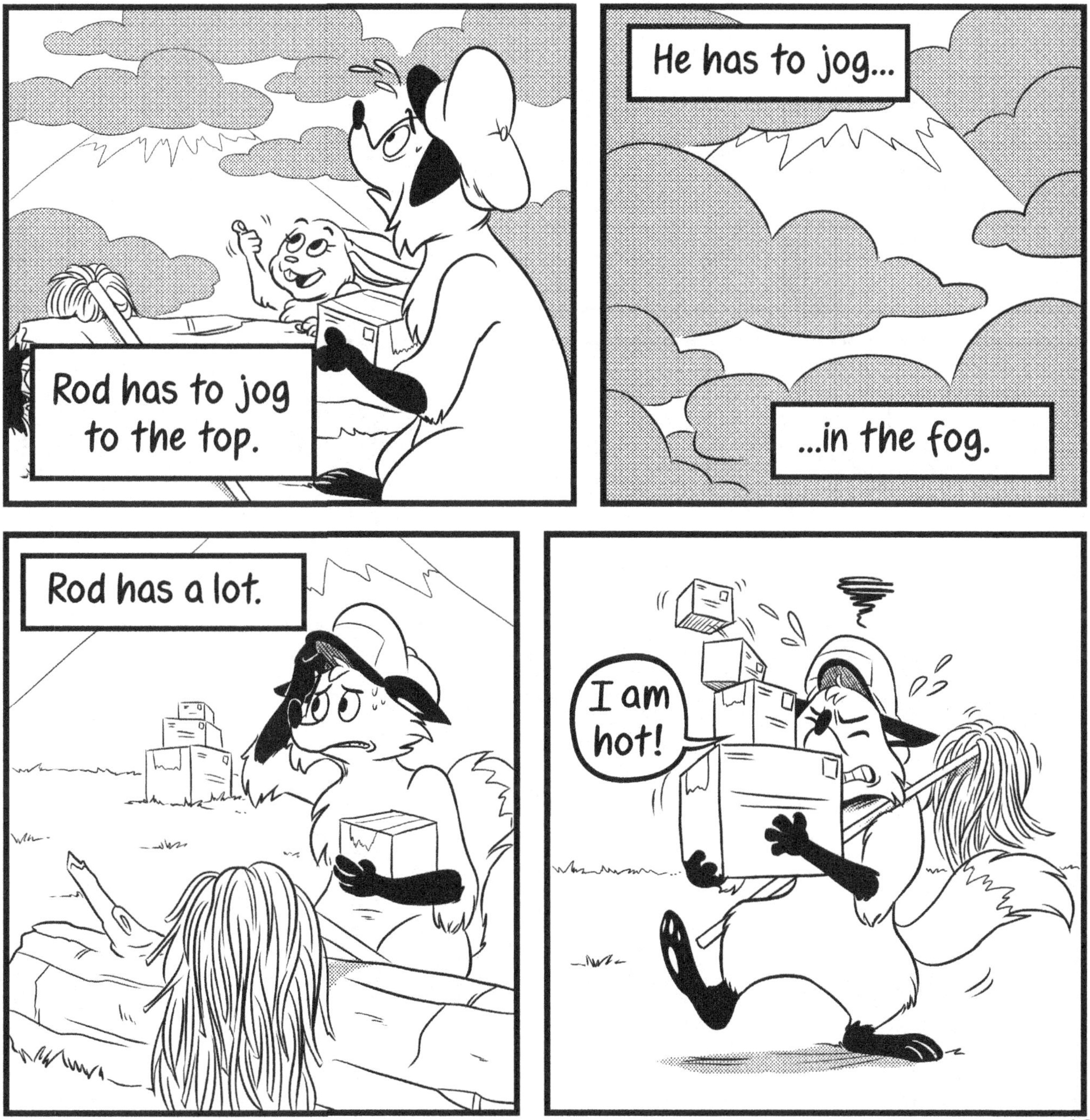
Rod has to jog to the top.
He has to jog...
...in the fog.
Rod has a lot.
I am hot!

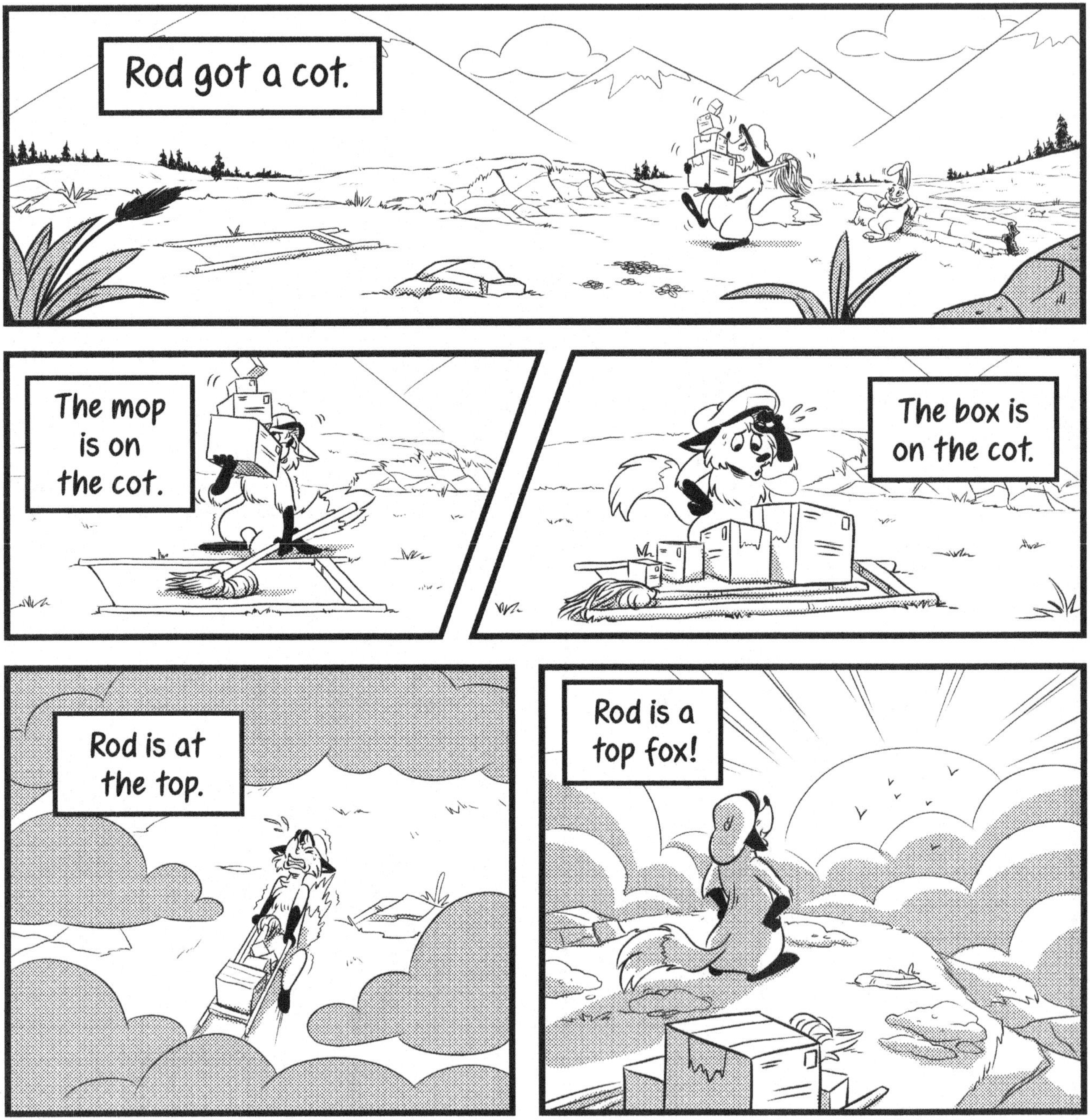
Rod got a cot.
The mop is on the cot.
The box is on the cot.
Rod is at the top.
Rod is a top fox!

# After You Read: Rod Has a Job

## CHECK FOR UNDERSTANDING

1. Where does Rod have to jog?
2. What does Rod pull to the top of the mountain?
3. How does Rod feel at the top of the mountain?
4. What will Rod do now that he is at the top of the mountain?

## PHONOLOGICAL AWARENESS SKILLS

1. What is a word that rhymes with "jog"?
2. What do you get if you blend the sounds /t/ /o/ /p/?
3. How many sounds do you hear in the word "fox"?
4. Can you change the first sound in "hot" to /p/? What's the new word?

STORY 3

# Pip's Kids

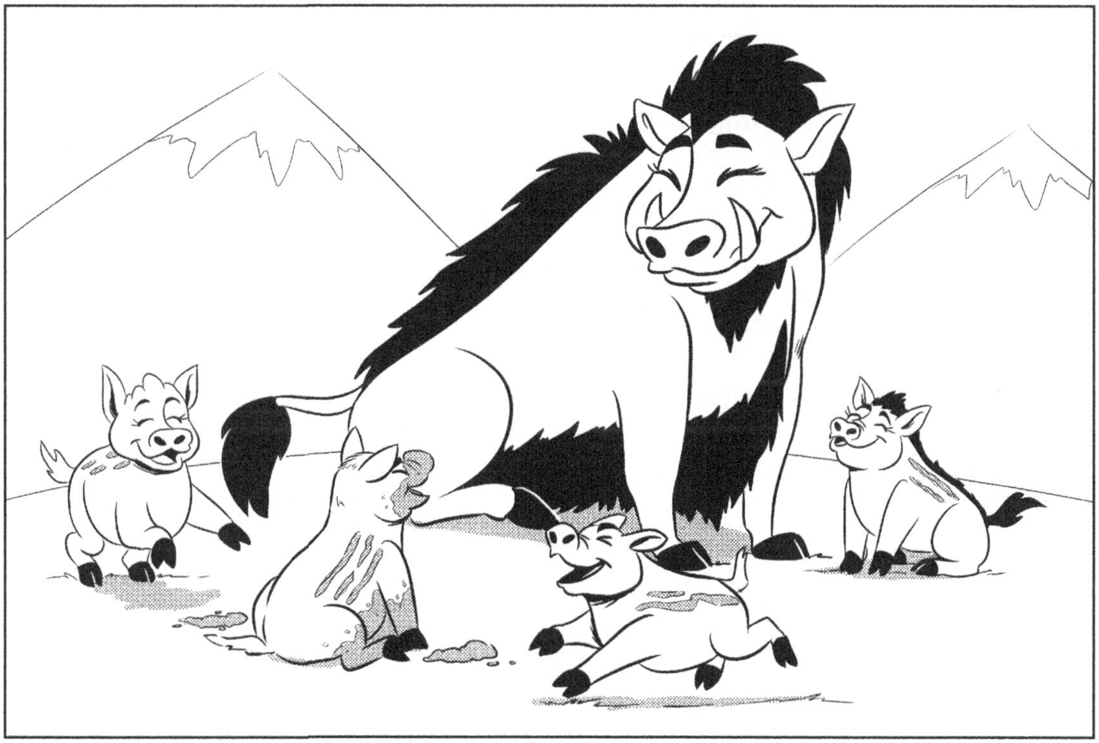

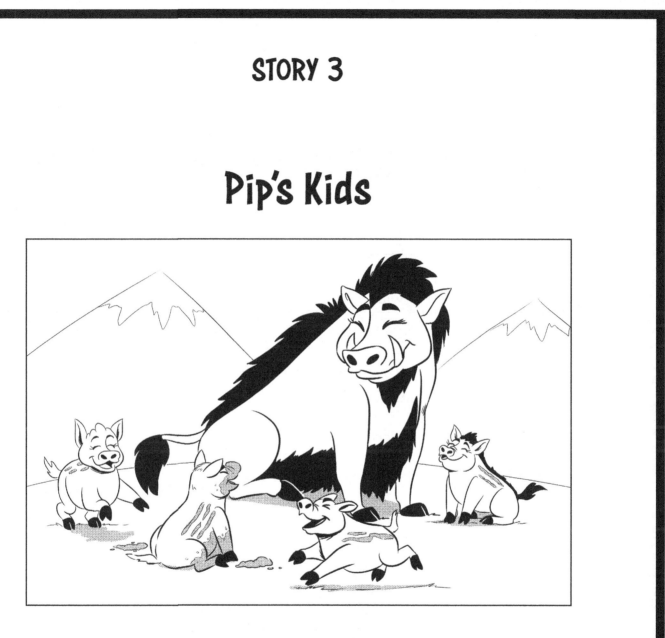

## SHORT I

# In This Story: Pip's Kids

| Skill Practiced: Short I | | | | | | |
|---|---|---|---|---|---|---|
| -ix | -ip | -ig | -id | -it | -im | -in |
| fix | Pip | pig | kids | Kit | Jim | tin |
|  | rip | big | Sid | pit |  |  |
|  | tips | Zig | did | sit |  |  |
|  |  | wig | lid | hit |  |  |
|  |  | digs | hid | sits |  |  |
|  |  | jig |  |  |  |  |
|  |  | pigs |  |  |  |  |

| Sight Words Covered | | |
|---|---|---|
| is | and | in |
| a | do |  |
| the | has |  |

Short I makes the sound /i/, as in *insect*.

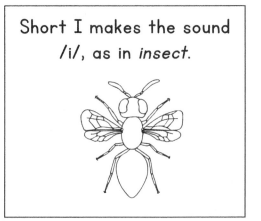

## Skills Learned Previously: Short A, Short O

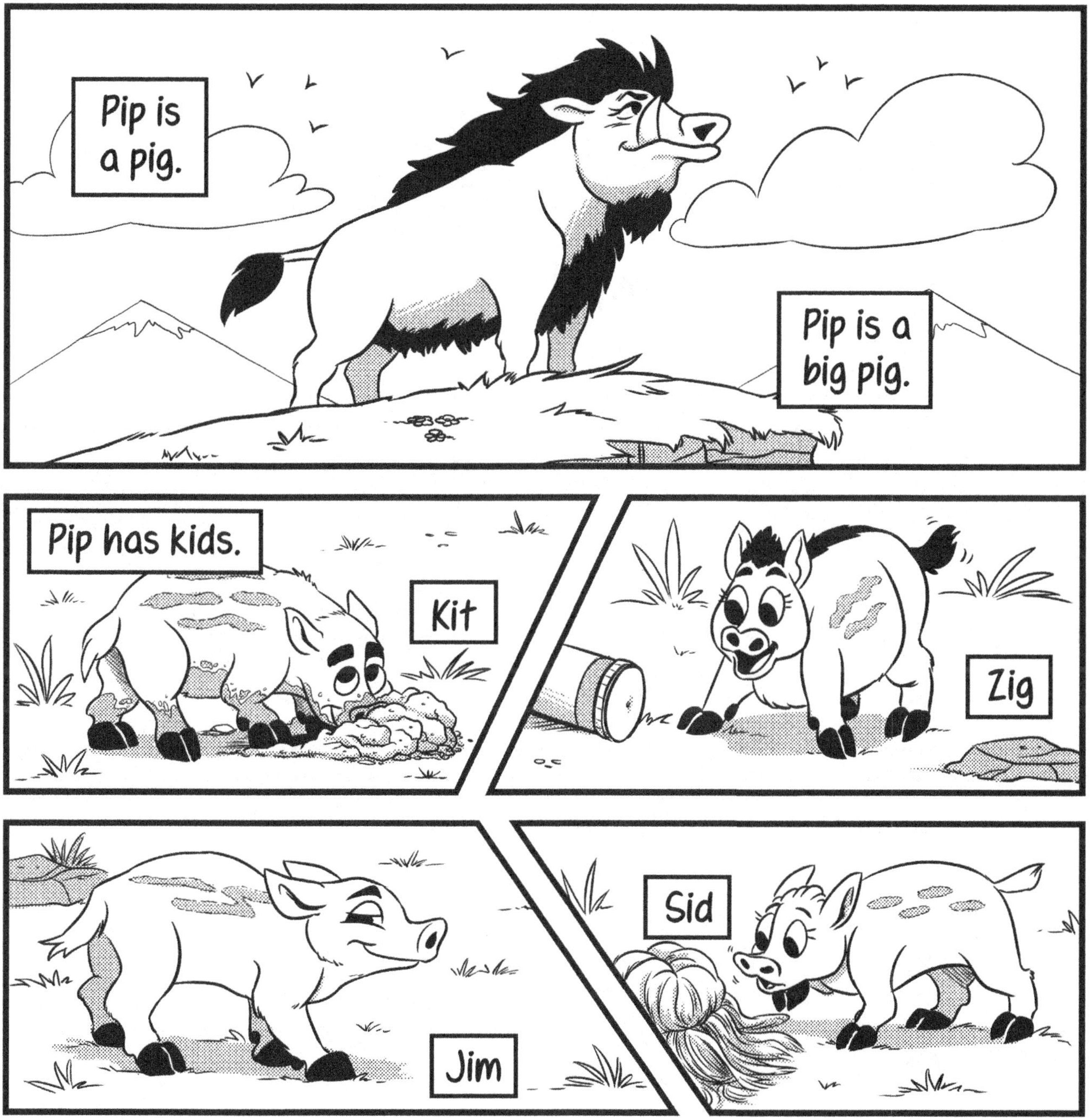

Pip is a pig.
Pip is a big pig.
Pip has kids.
Kit
Zig
Jim
Sid

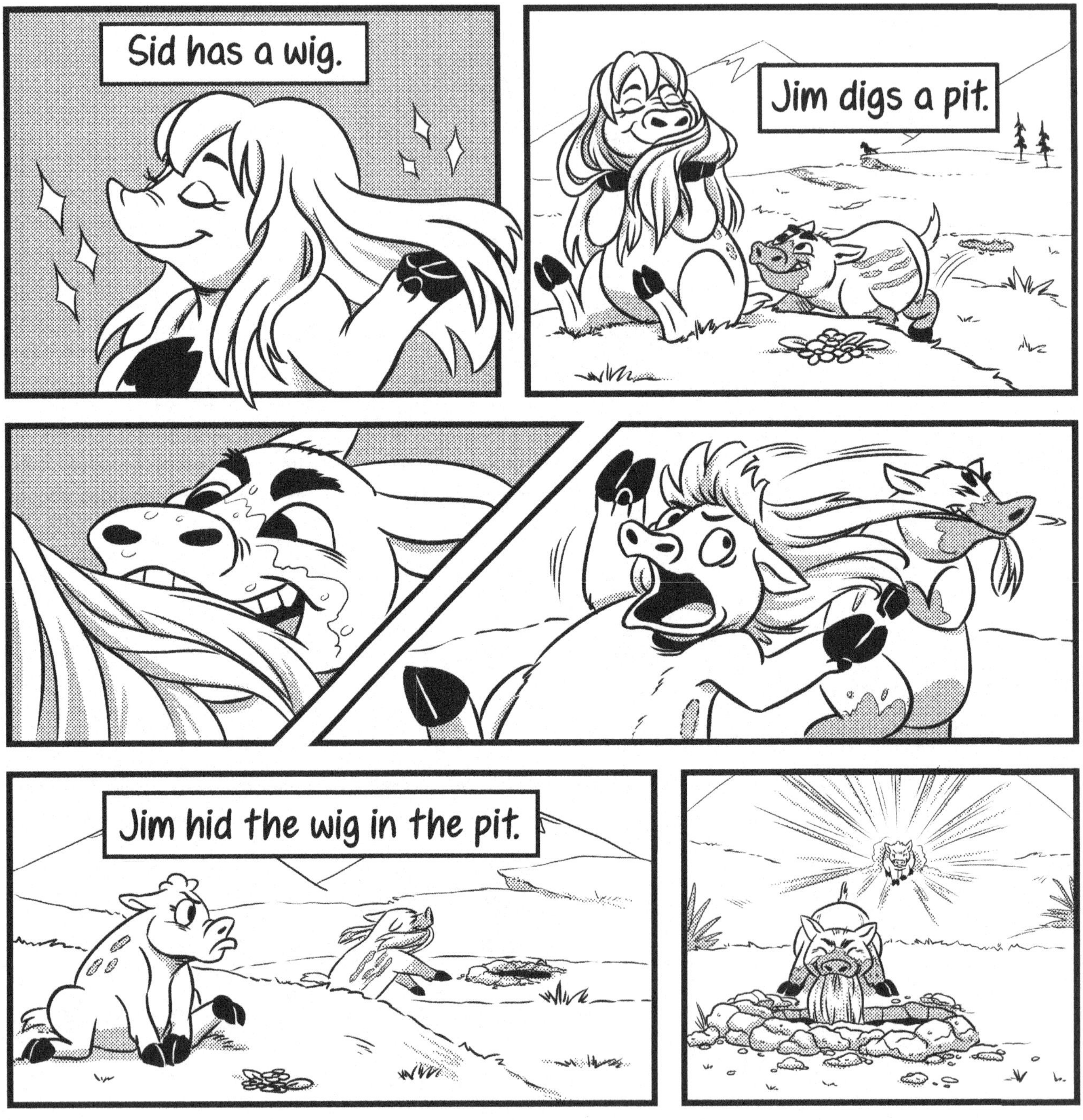
Sid has a wig.
Jim digs a pit.
Jim hid the wig in the pit.

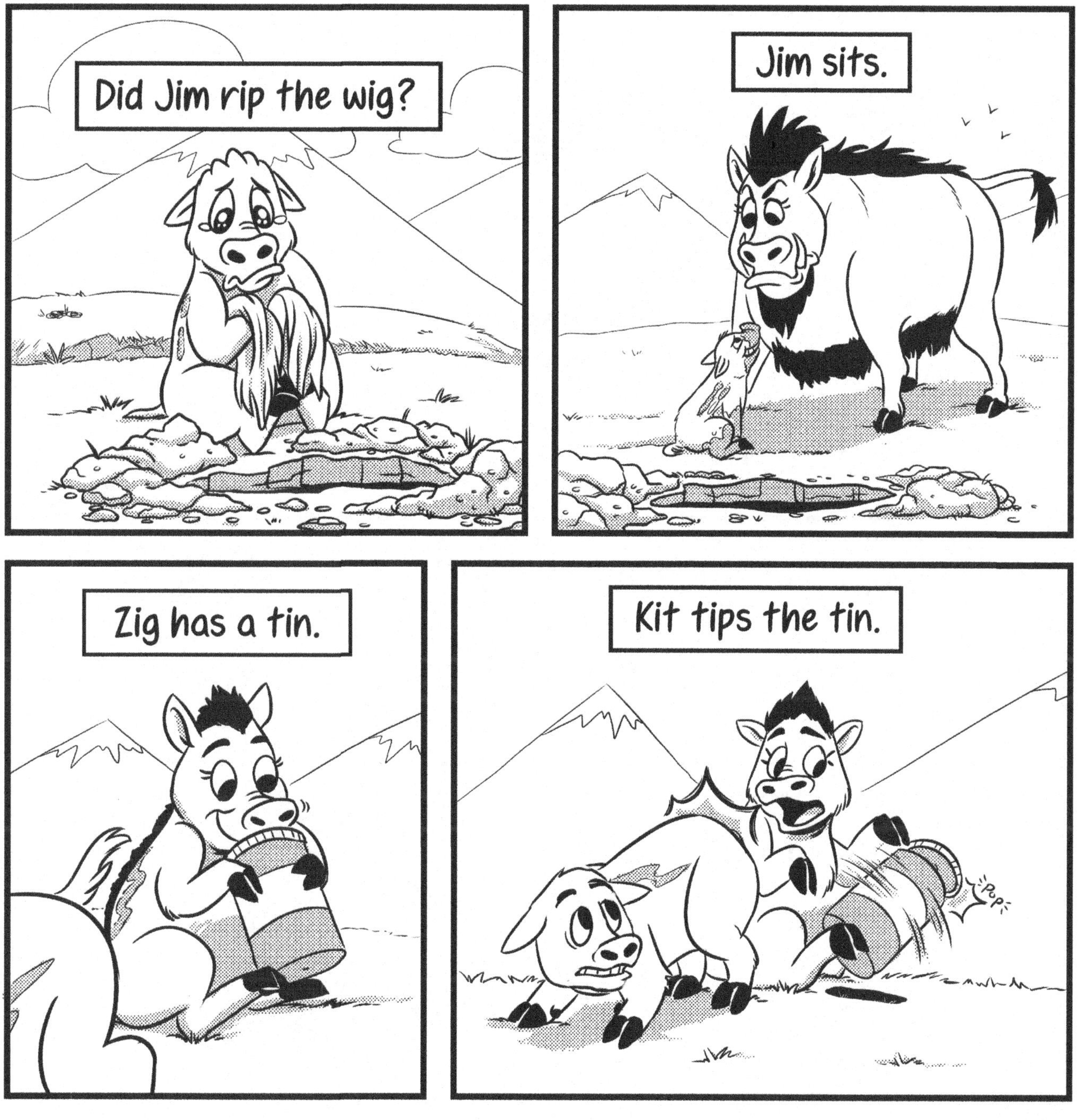
Did Jim rip the wig?
Jim sits.
Zig has a tin.
Kit tips the tin.
Pop

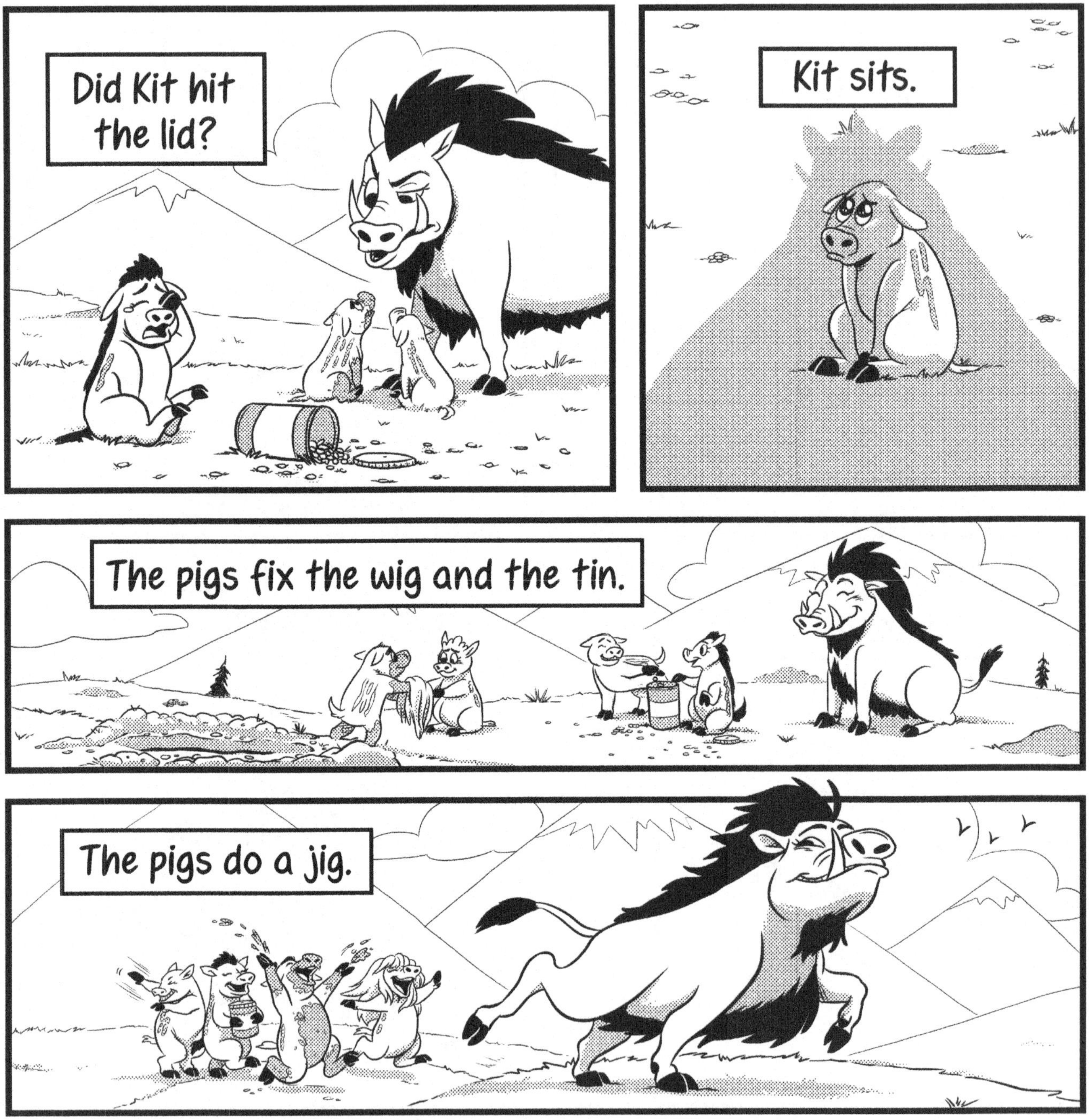
Did Kit hit the lid?
Kit sits.
The pigs fix the wig and the tin.
The pigs do a jig.

# After You Read: Pip's Kids

## CHECK FOR UNDERSTANDING

1. What does Sid have?
2. Where did Jim hide the wig?
3. How does Pip the pig feel about how her kids are behaving?
4. What are some other silly things Pip's kids might do?

## PHONOLOGICAL AWARENESS SKILLS

1. What is a word that rhymes with *"wig"*?
2. What do you get if you blend the sounds /f/ /i/ /x/?
3. How many sounds do you hear in the word *"sit"*?
4. Can you change the first sound in *"hid"* to /l/? What's the new word?

## STORY 4

# The Bad Bet

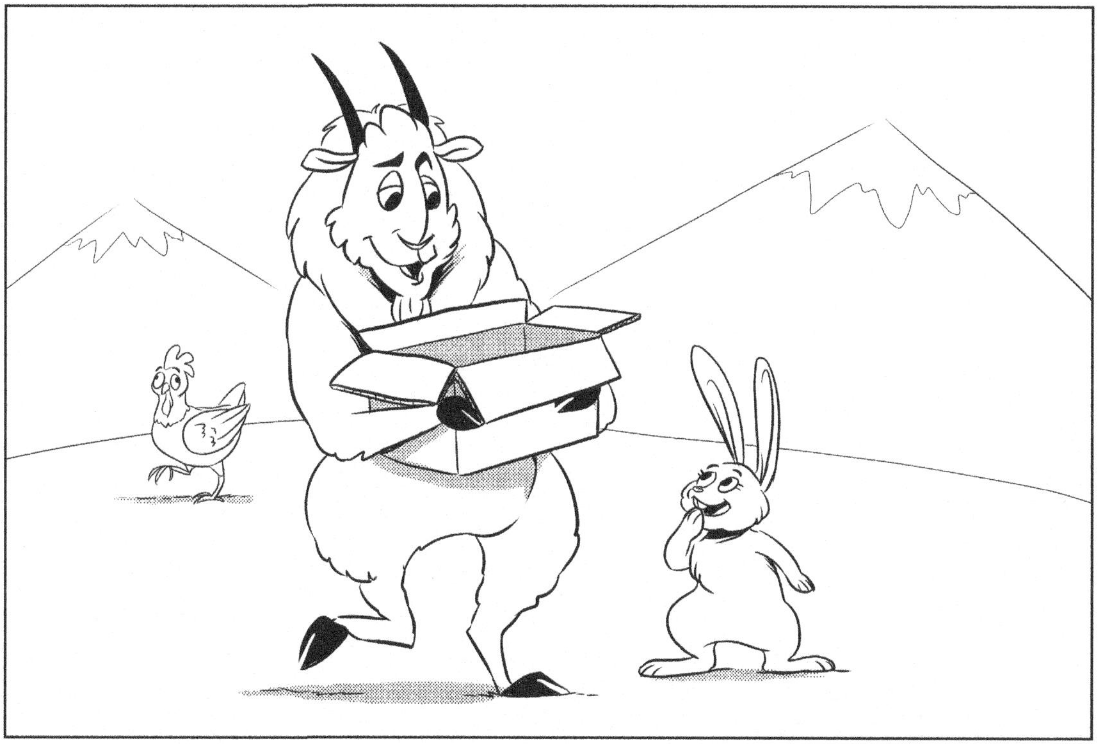

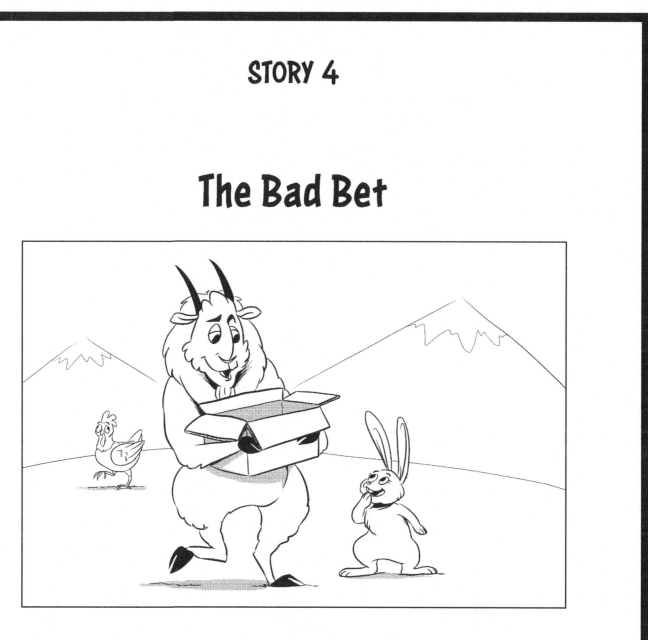

## SHORT E

# In This Story: The Bad Bet

| Skill Practiced: Short E | | | | |
|---|---|---|---|---|
| -eg | -en | -et | -es | -ed |
| Meg | Ren | bet | yes | red |
| pegs | ten | get | | led |
| peg | hen | gets | | |
| leg | | net | | |
| | | yet | | |
| | | wet | | |
| | | lets | | |
| | | vet | | |
| | | pet | | |

| Sight Words Covered | | |
|---|---|---|
| and | go | the |
| a | was | in |
| is | to | |

Short E makes the sound /e/, as in *egg*.

## Skills Learned Previously: Short A, Short O, Short I

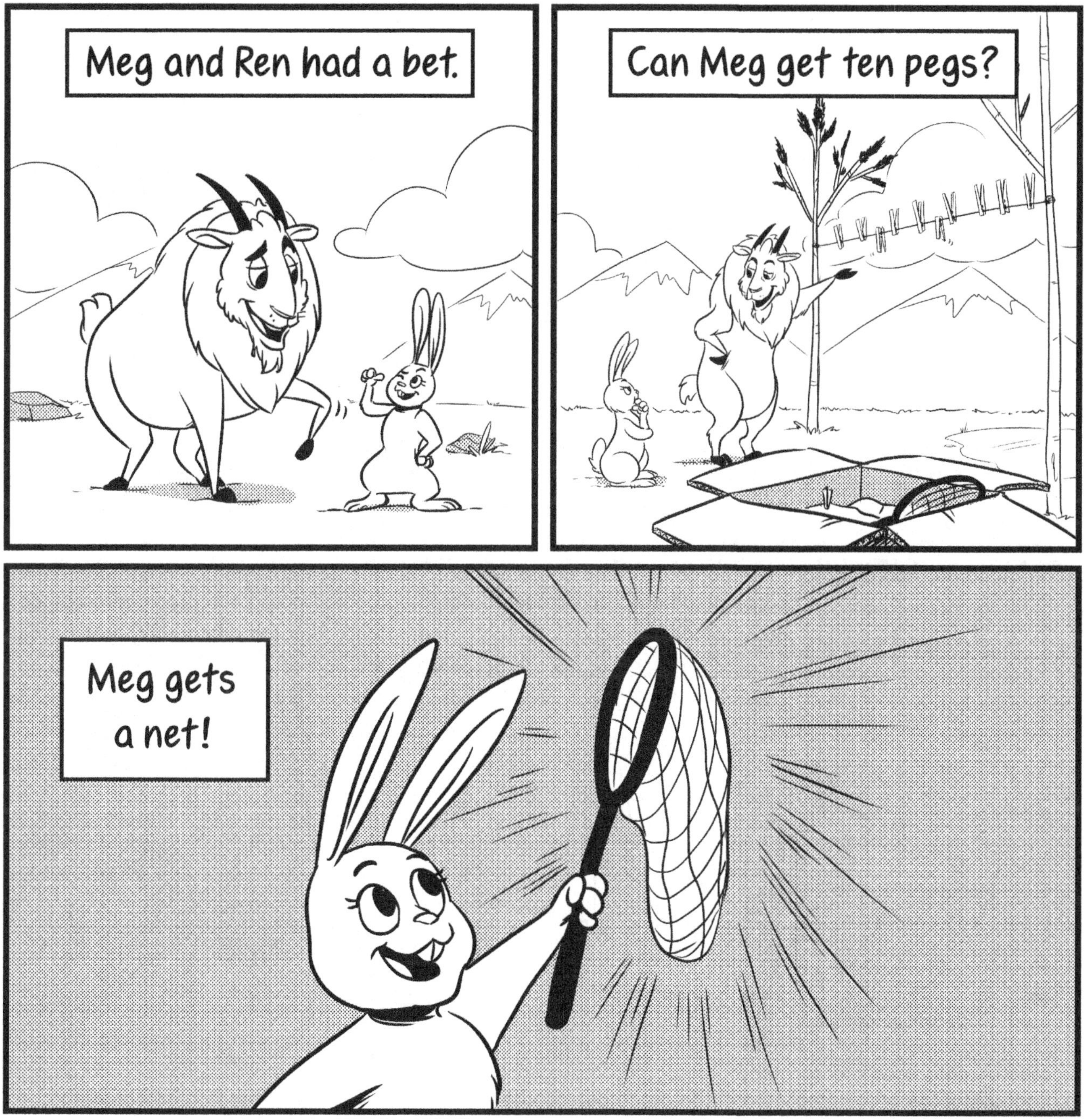
Meg and Ren had a bet.
Can Meg get ten pegs?
Meg gets a net!

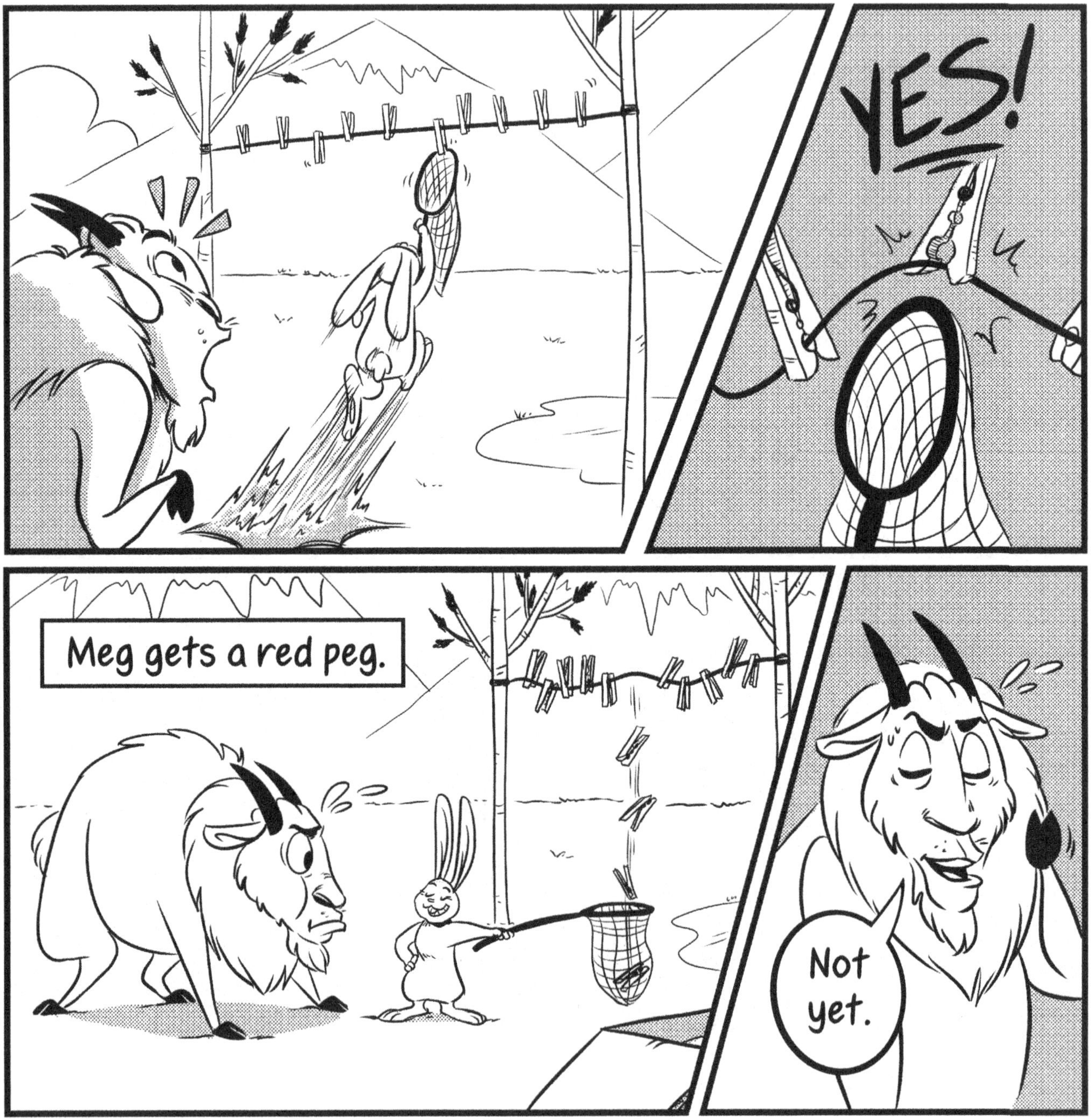
YES!
Meg gets a red peg.
Not yet.

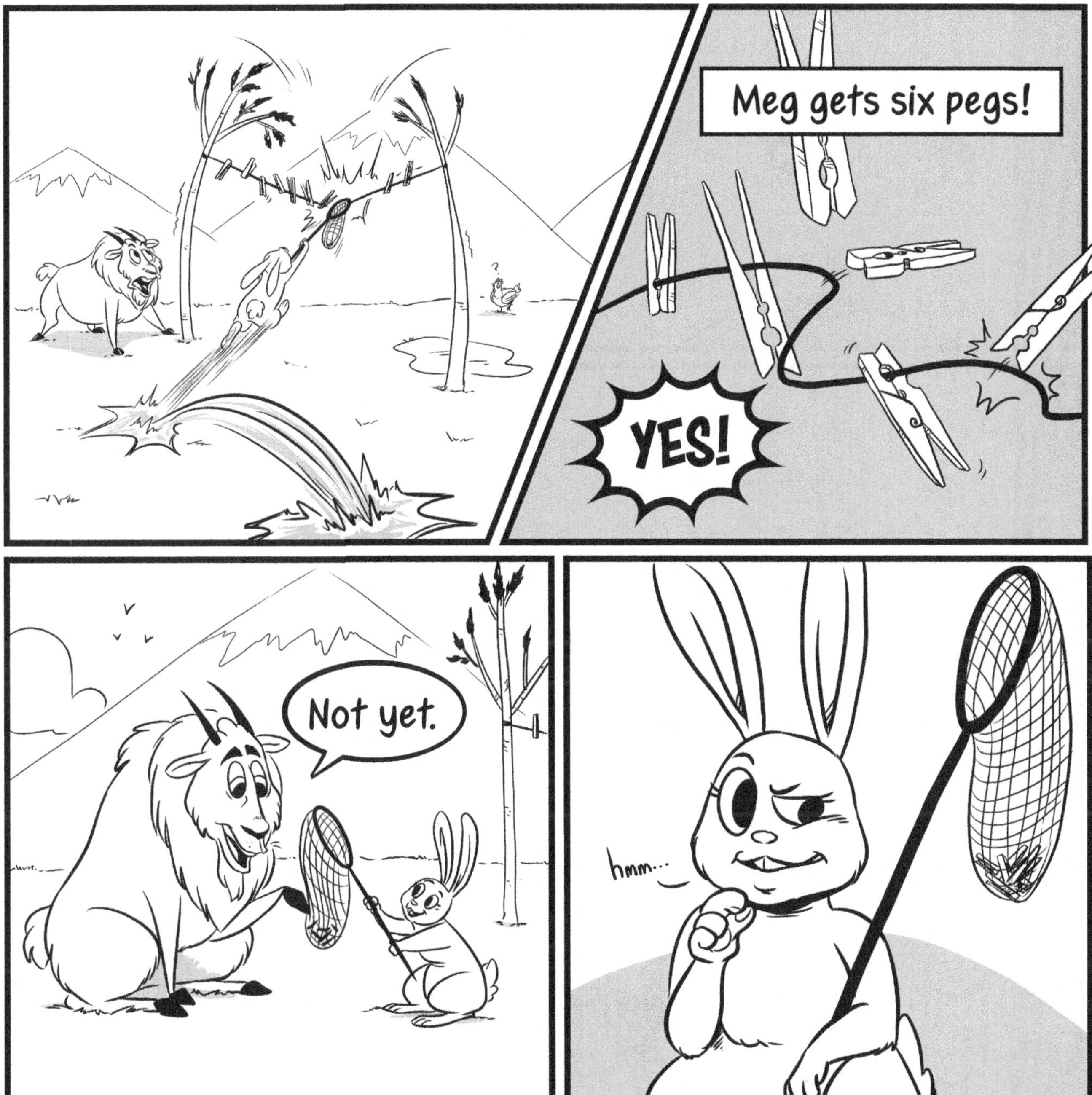
Meg gets six pegs!
YES!
Not yet.
hmm...

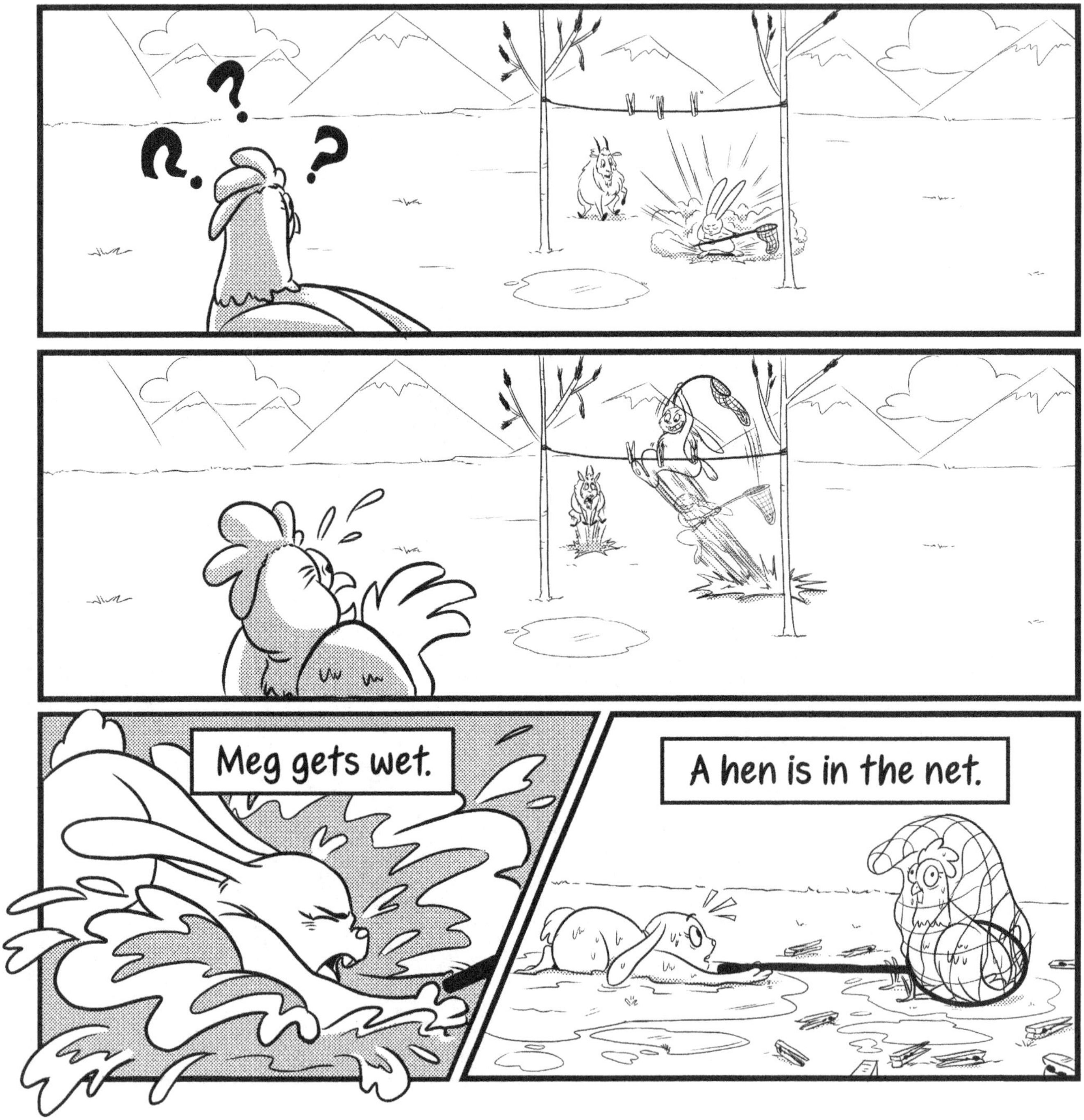
Meg gets wet.
A hen is in the net.

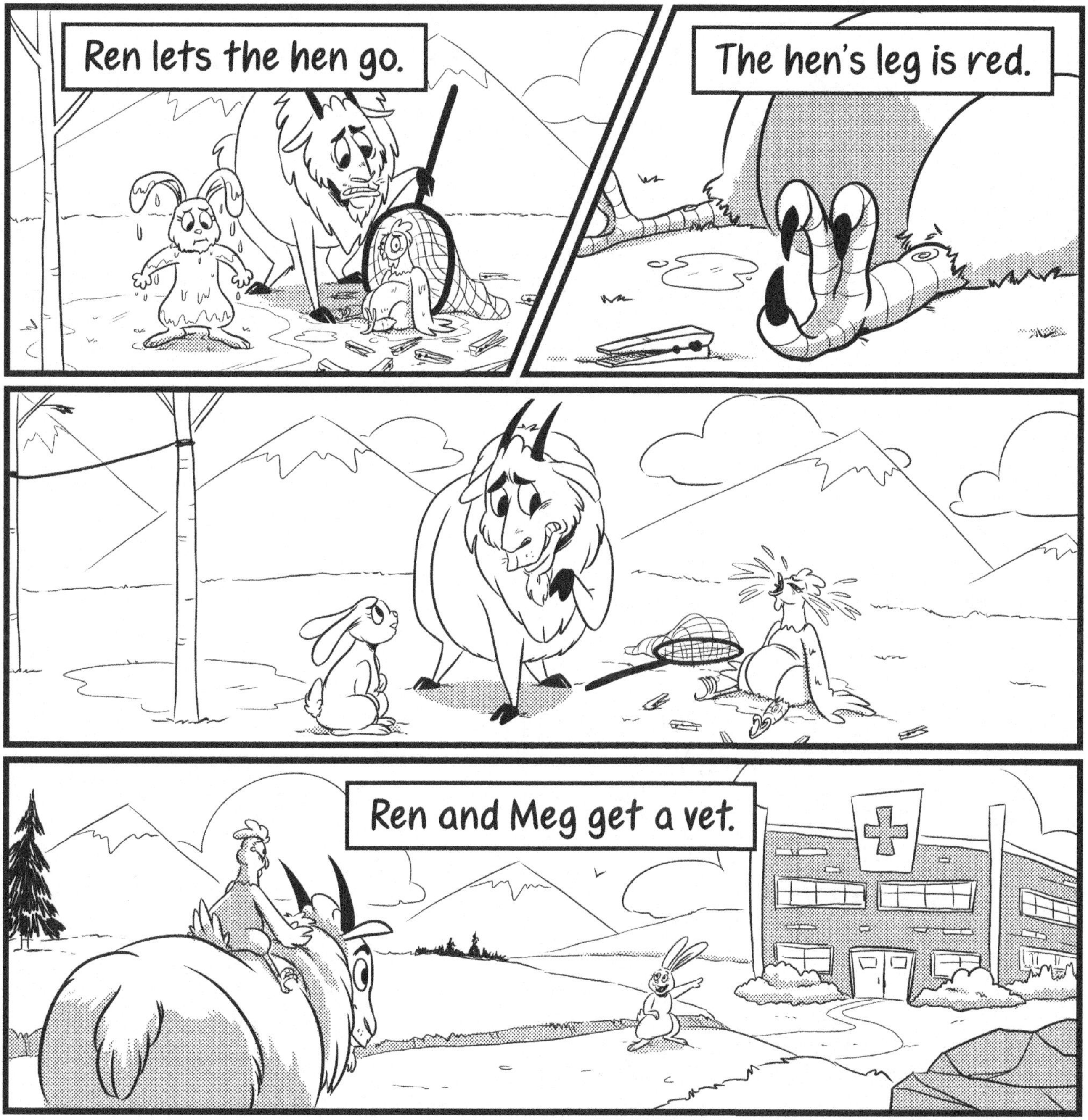
Ren lets the hen go.
The hen's leg is red.
Ren and Meg get a vet.

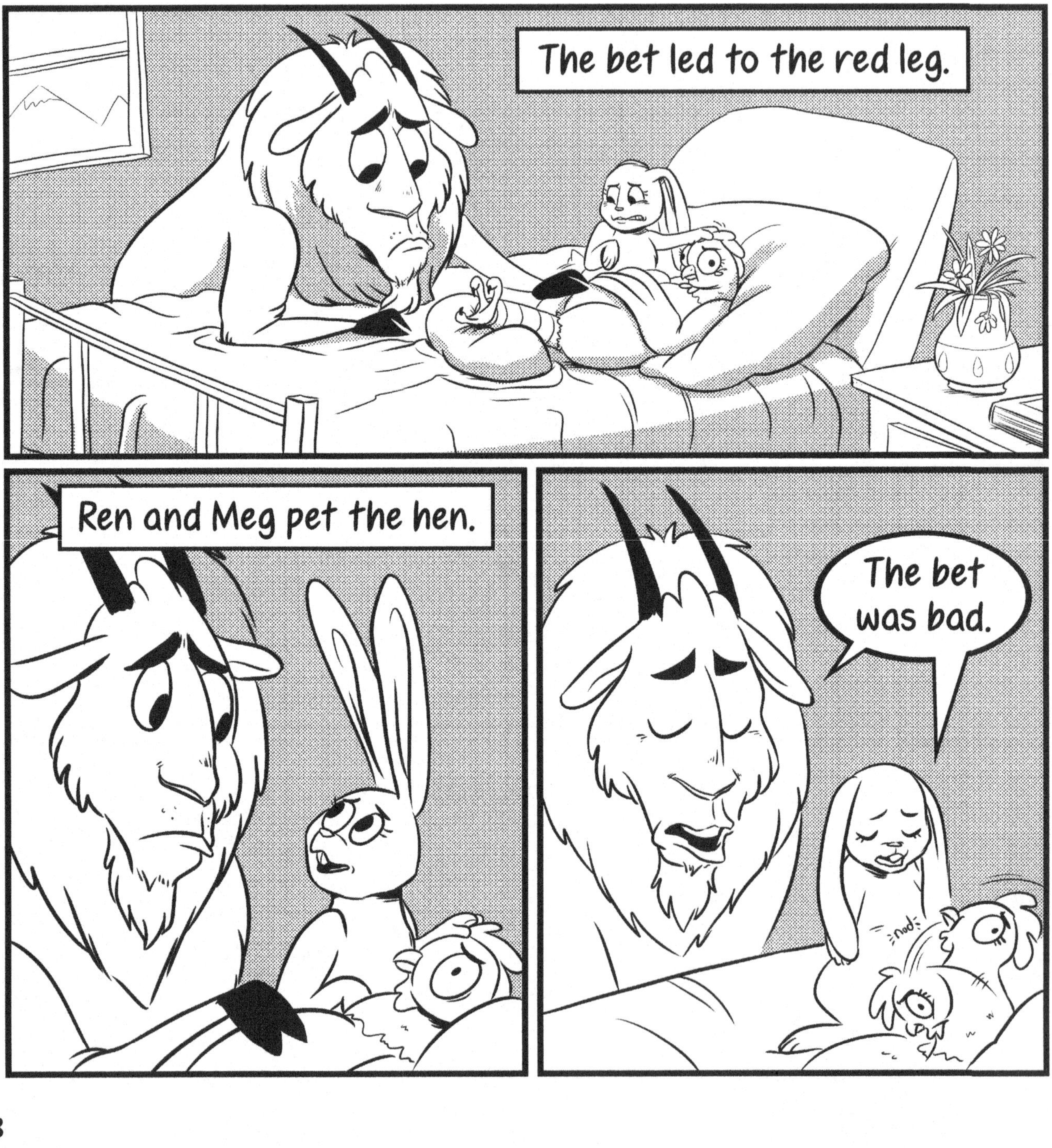
The bet led to the red leg.
Ren and Meg pet the hen.
The bet was bad.
nod

# After You Read: The Bad Bet

## CHECK FOR UNDERSTANDING

1. What did Ren bet Meg to do?
2. What gets caught in Meg's net?
3. How do Meg and Ren feel when the hen's leg is red?
4. Will Meg and Ren have more bets? Why or why not?

## PHONOLOGICAL AWARENESS SKILLS

1. What is a word that rhymes with "*bet?*"
2. What do you get if you blend the sounds /h/ /e/ /n/?
3. How many sounds do you hear in the word "yes"?
4. Can you change the first sound in "*red*" to /b/? What's the new word?

# STORY 5

# Gus and Jud

# SHORT U

# In This Story: Gus and Jud

| Skill Practiced: Short U | | | | | | | |
|---|---|---|---|---|---|---|---|
| -us | -ub | -ud | -up | -un | -ug | -ut | -um |
| Gus | cub | Jud | Pup | run | tug | cut | mum |
|  | tub | mud |  | fun | hug | but |  |
|  |  |  |  | sun |  |  |  |
|  |  |  |  | runs |  |  |  |

| Sight Words Covered | | |
|---|---|---|
| is | and | to |
| a | too | in |
| the | it | his |

Short U makes the sound /u/, as in *umbrella*.

Skills Learned Previously: Short A, Short O, Short I, Short E

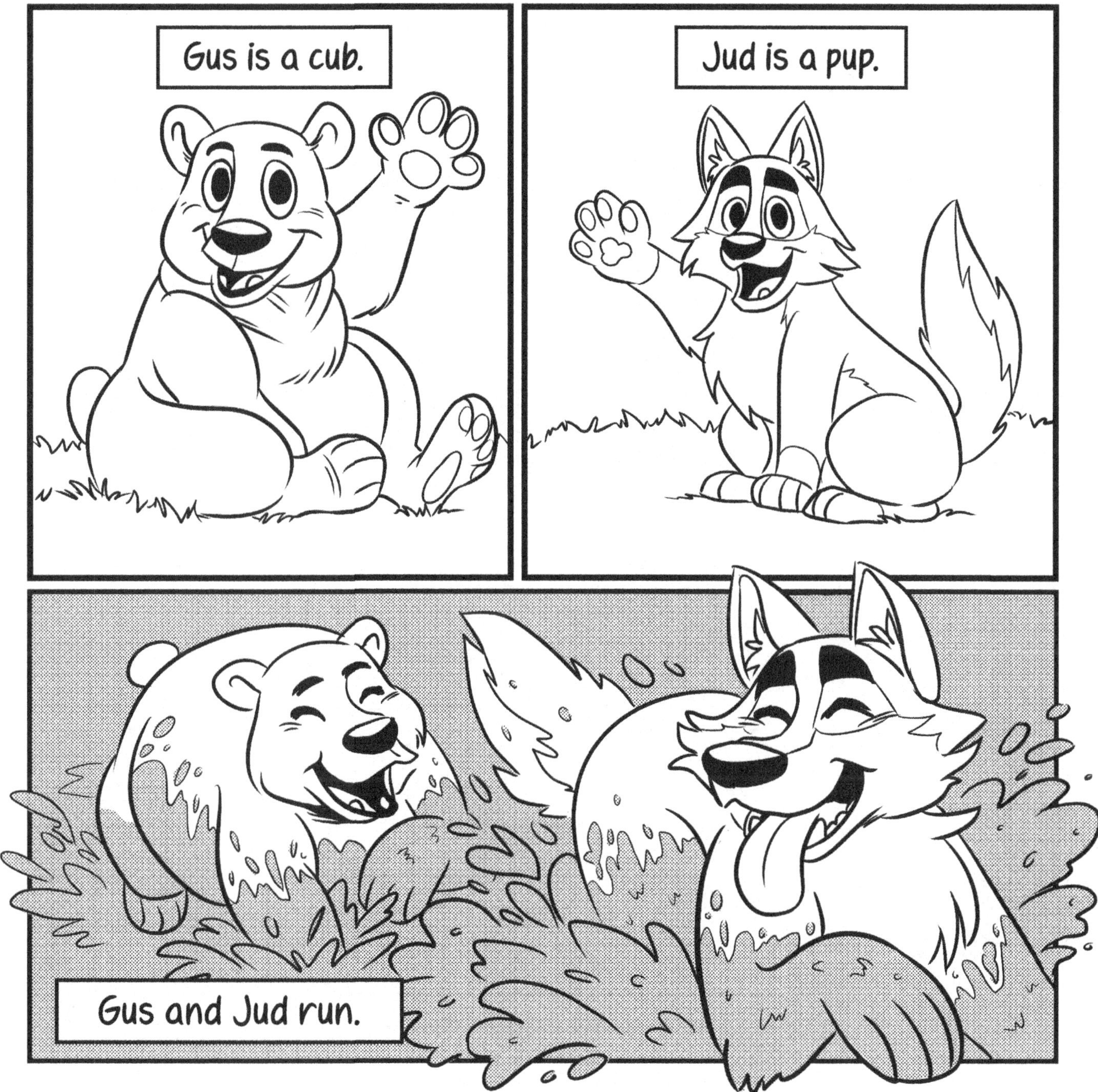
Gus is a cub.
Jud is a pup.
Gus and Jud run.

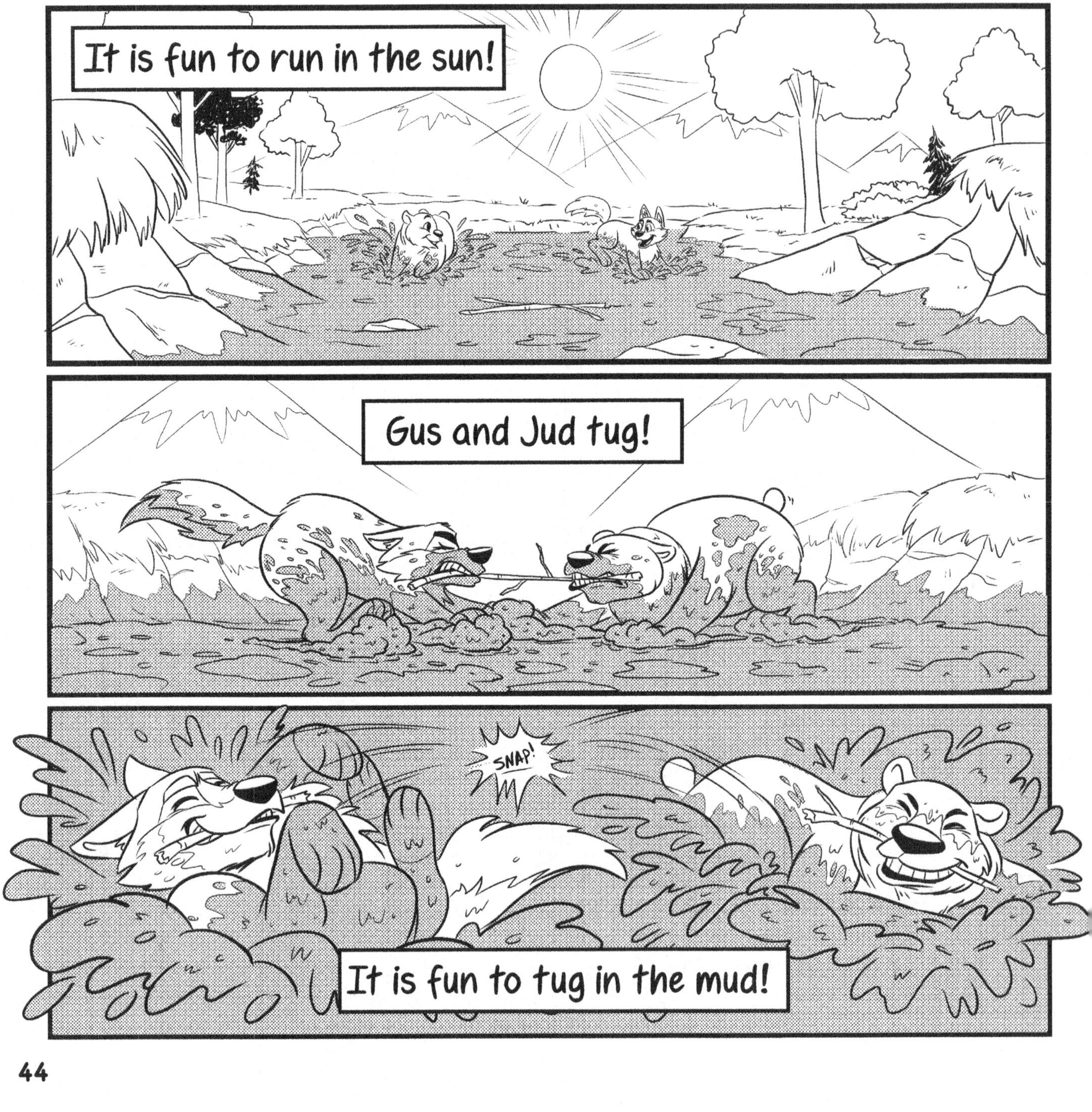
It is fun to run in the sun!
Gus and Jud tug!
SNAP!
It is fun to tug in the mud!

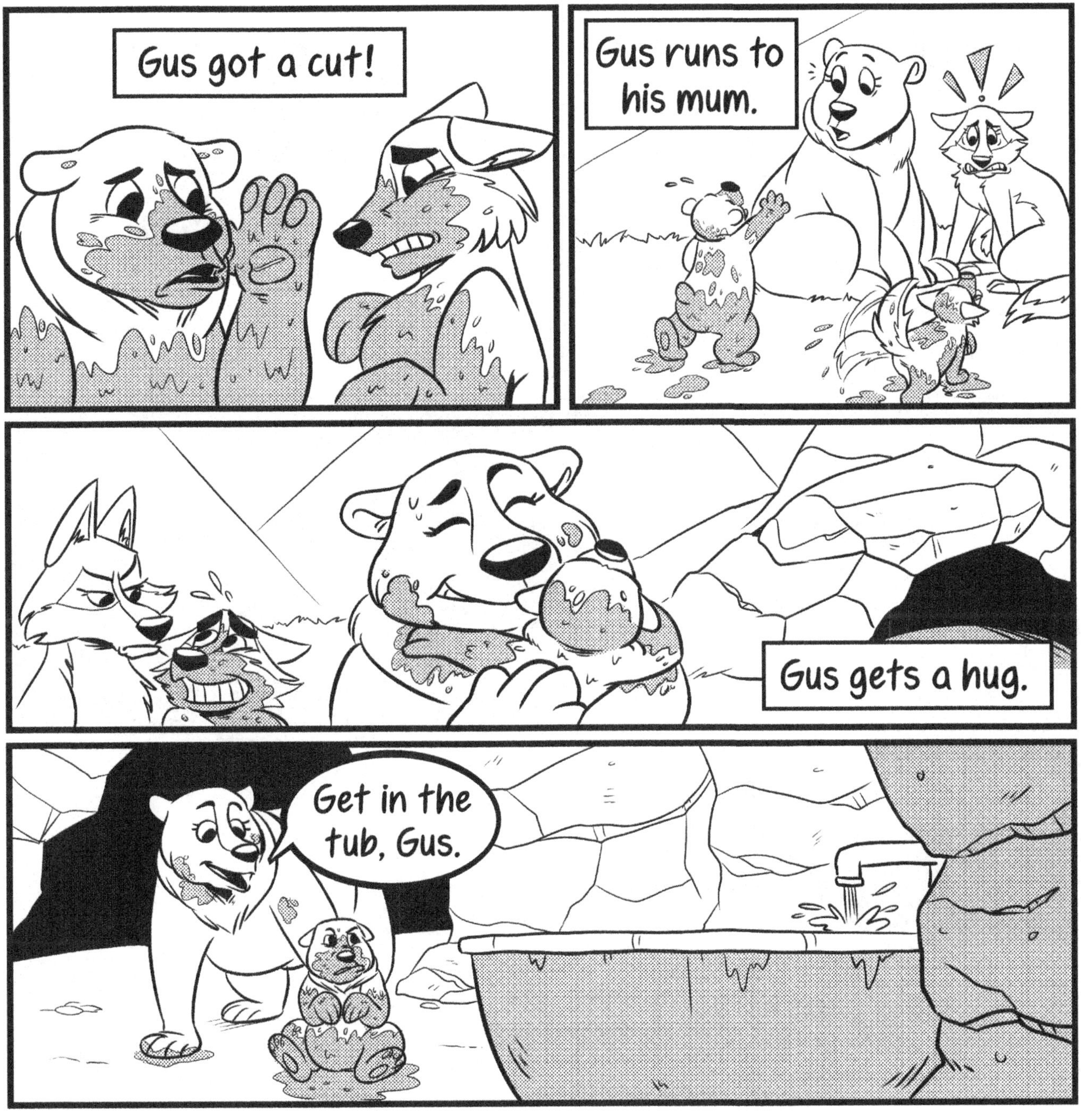

Gus got a cut!
Gus runs to his mum.
Gus gets a hug.
Get in the tub, Gus.

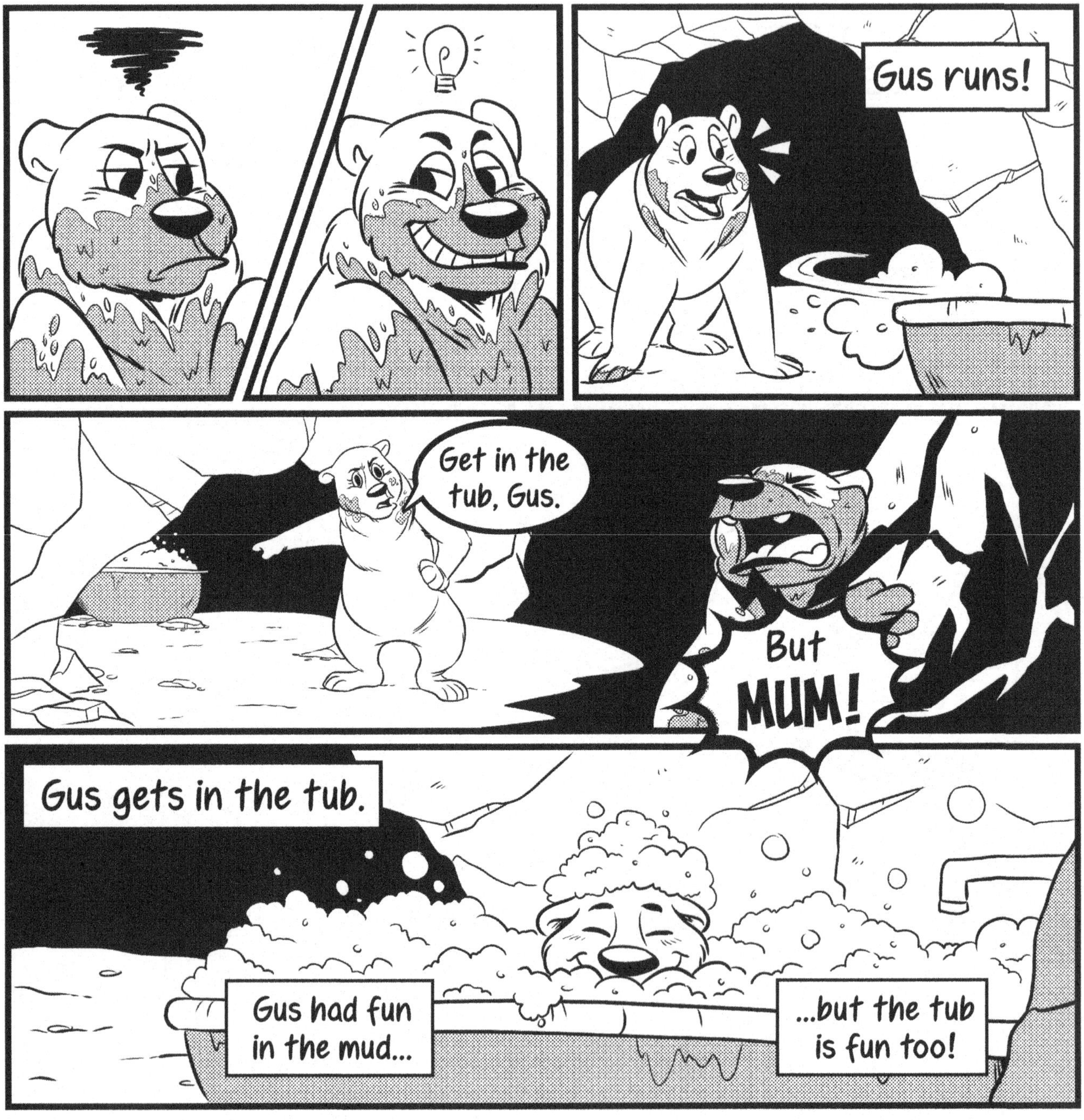
Gus runs!
Get in the tub, Gus.
But MUM!
Gus gets in the tub.
Gus had fun in the mud...
...but the tub is fun too!

# After You Read: Gus and Jud

## CHECK FOR UNDERSTANDING

1. What happened to Gus in the mud?
2. How do you think Gus got the cut?
3. Why doesn't Gus want to get in the tub?
4. What will Gus and Jud do after Gus's bath?

## PHONOLOGICAL AWARENESS SKILLS

1. What is a word that rhymes with "*fun*"?
2. What do you get if you blend the sounds /t/ /u/ /g/?
3. How many sounds do you hear in the word "*pup*"?
4. Can you change the first sound in "*but*" to /r/? What's the new word?

# STORY 6

# Rod Gets a Cut

## ALL SHORT VOWELS

# In This Story: Rod Gets a Cut

| Skill Practiced: All Short Vowels | | | | |
|---|---|---|---|---|
| Short A | Short E | Short I | Short O | Short U |
| Zak | den | sit | Rod | hut |
| yak | ten | sip | fox | cut |
| has | leg | hit | jog | run |
| had | let | him | job | rubs |
| sad | yet | fit | log | but |
| can | yes | kit | hop | bus |
|  |  | did | top |  |
|  |  | fix | not |  |
|  |  |  | got |  |

| Sight Words Covered | | | |
|---|---|---|---|
| he | and | to | I |
| a | is | on | you |
| the | it | was | his |

## Skills Learned Previously: Short A, Short E, Short I, Short U, Short O

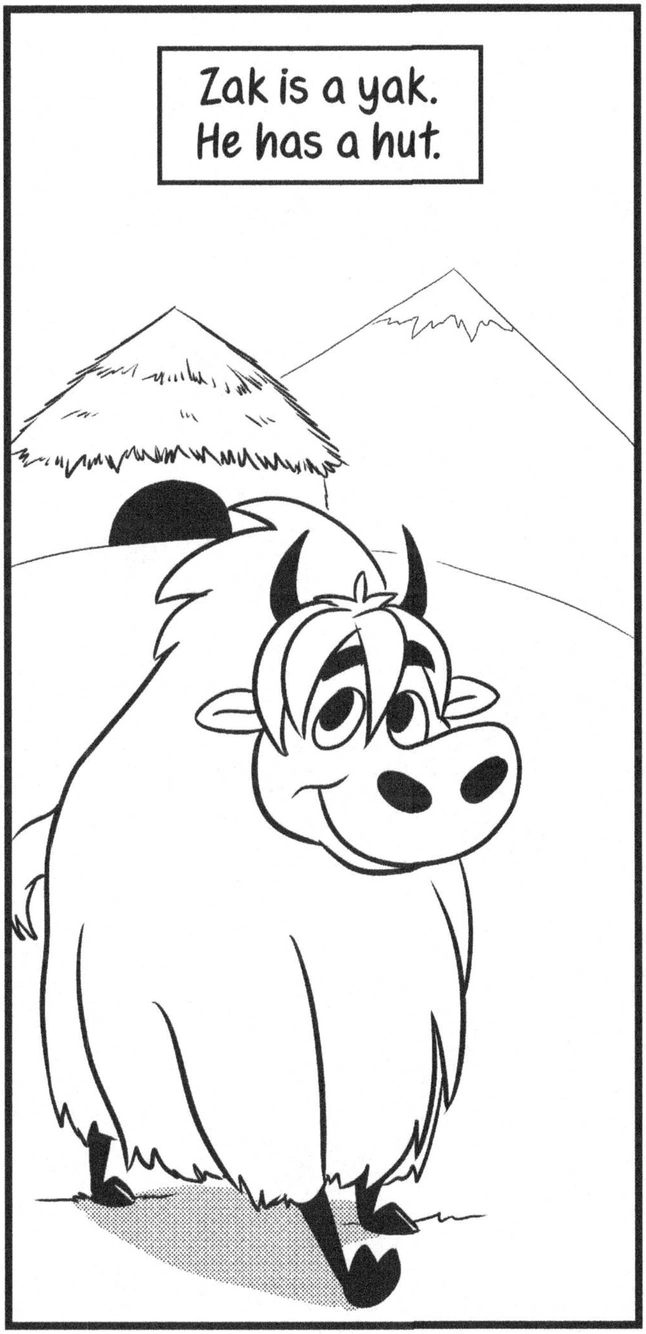
Zak is a yak.
He has a hut.

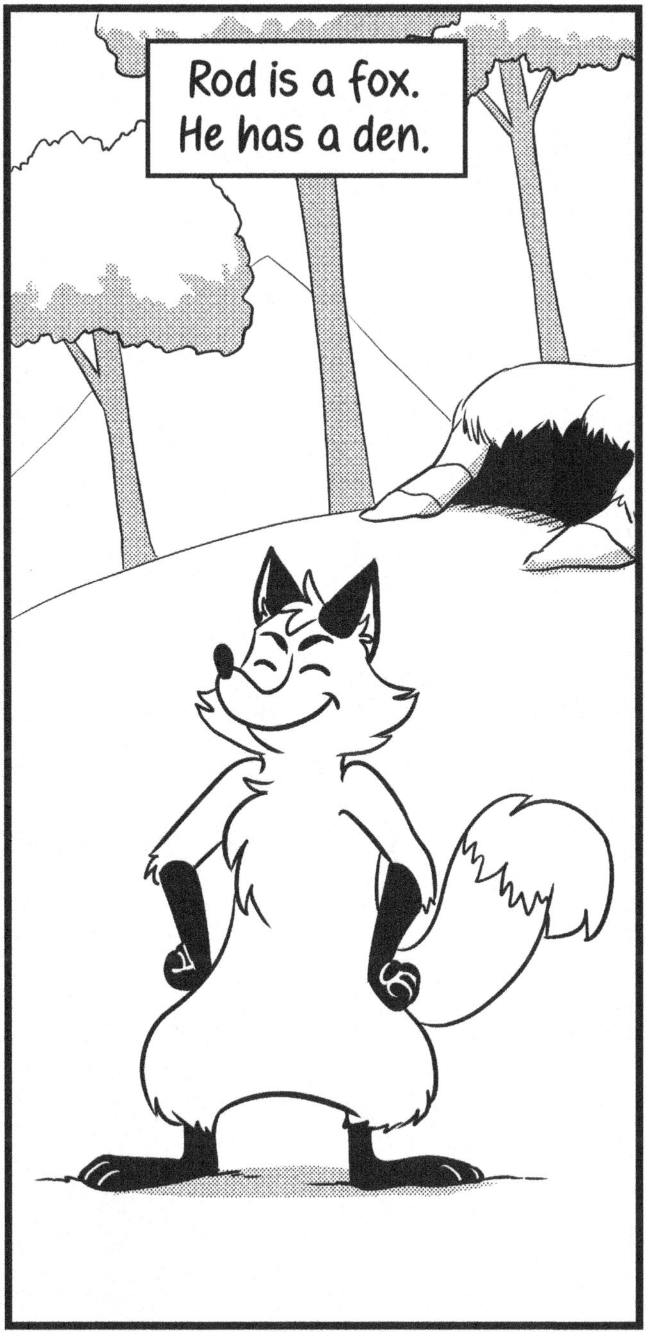
Rod is a fox.
He has a den.

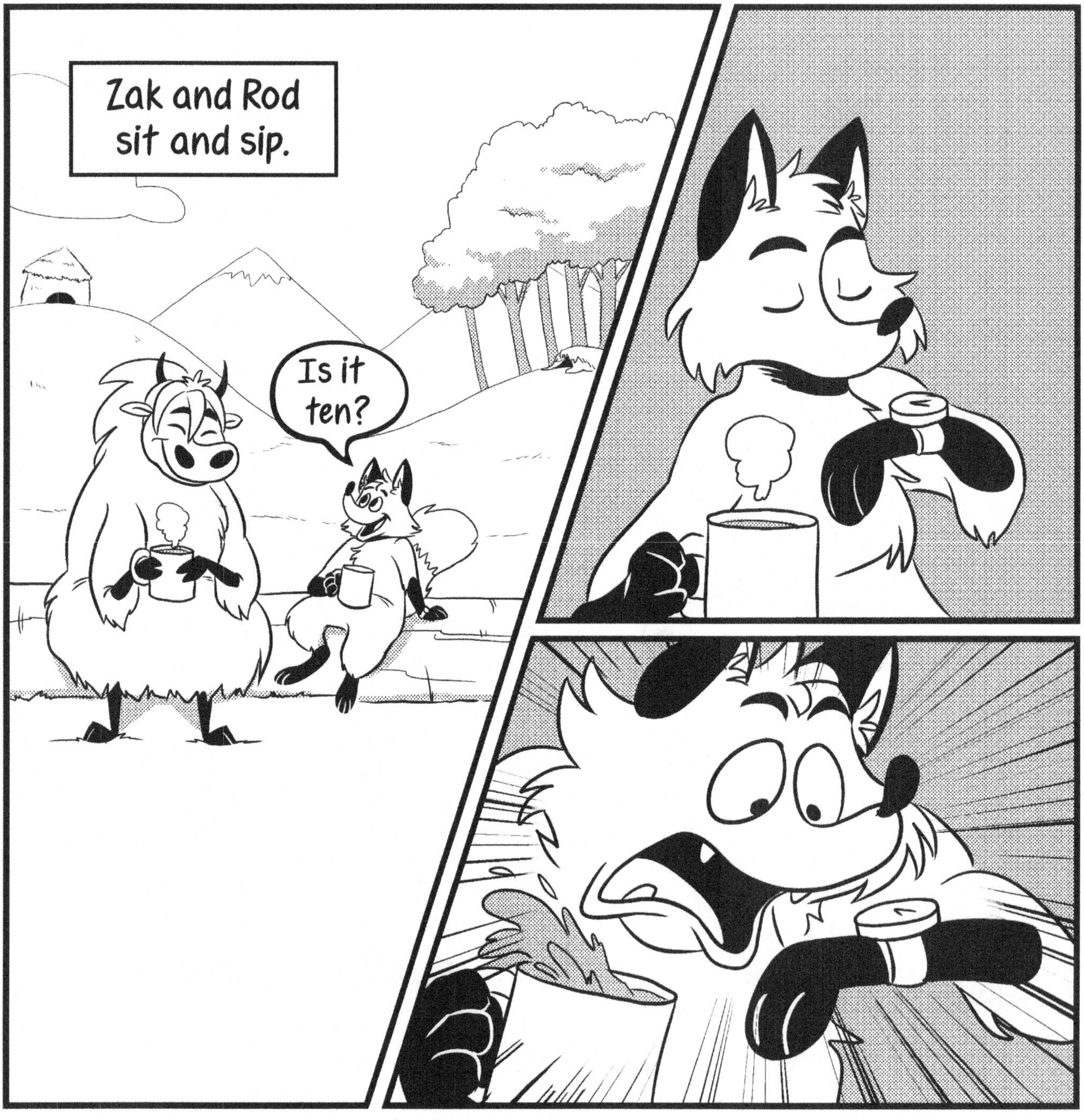
Zak and Rod
sit and sip.
Is it
ten?

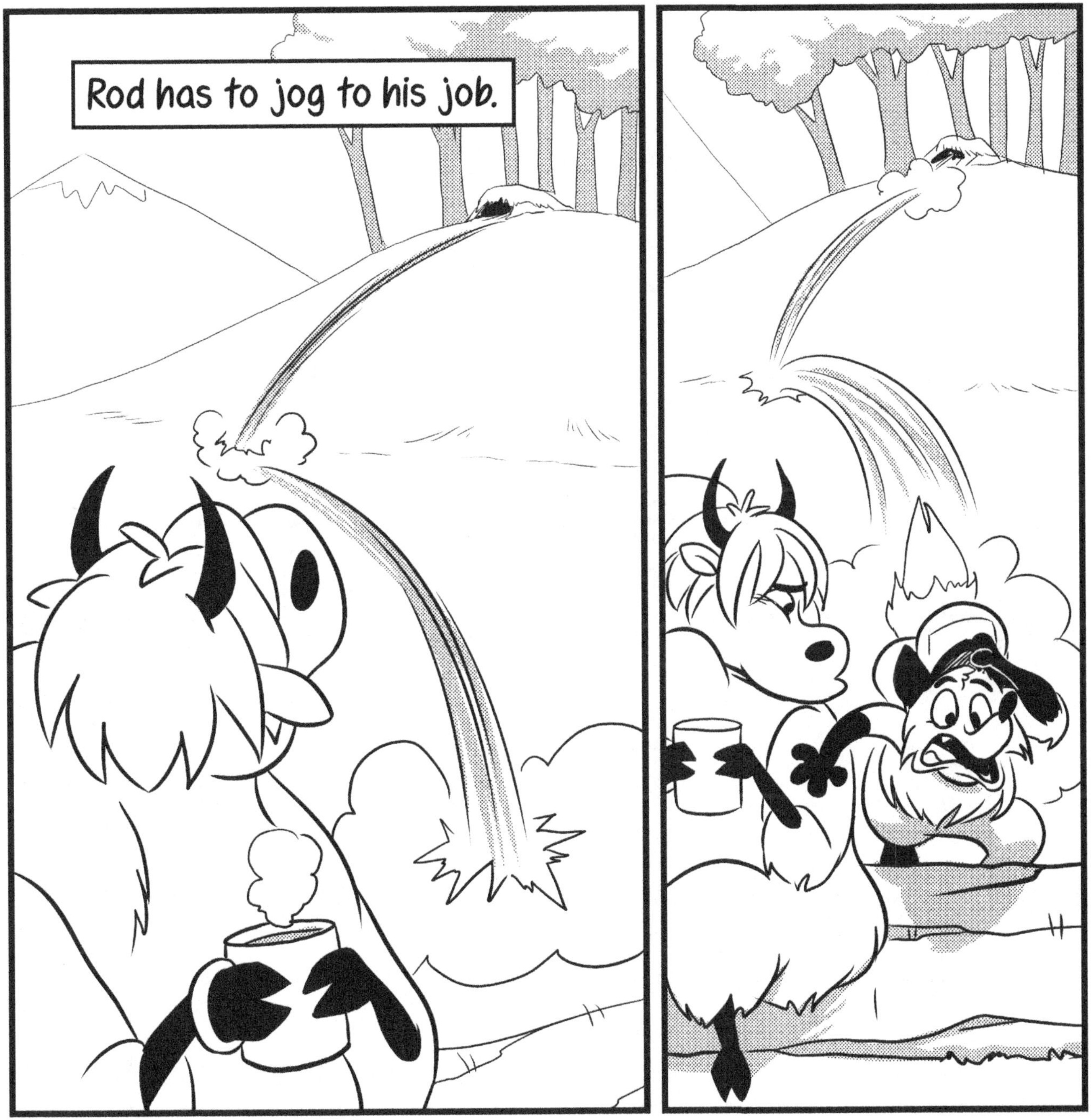
Rod has to jog to his job.

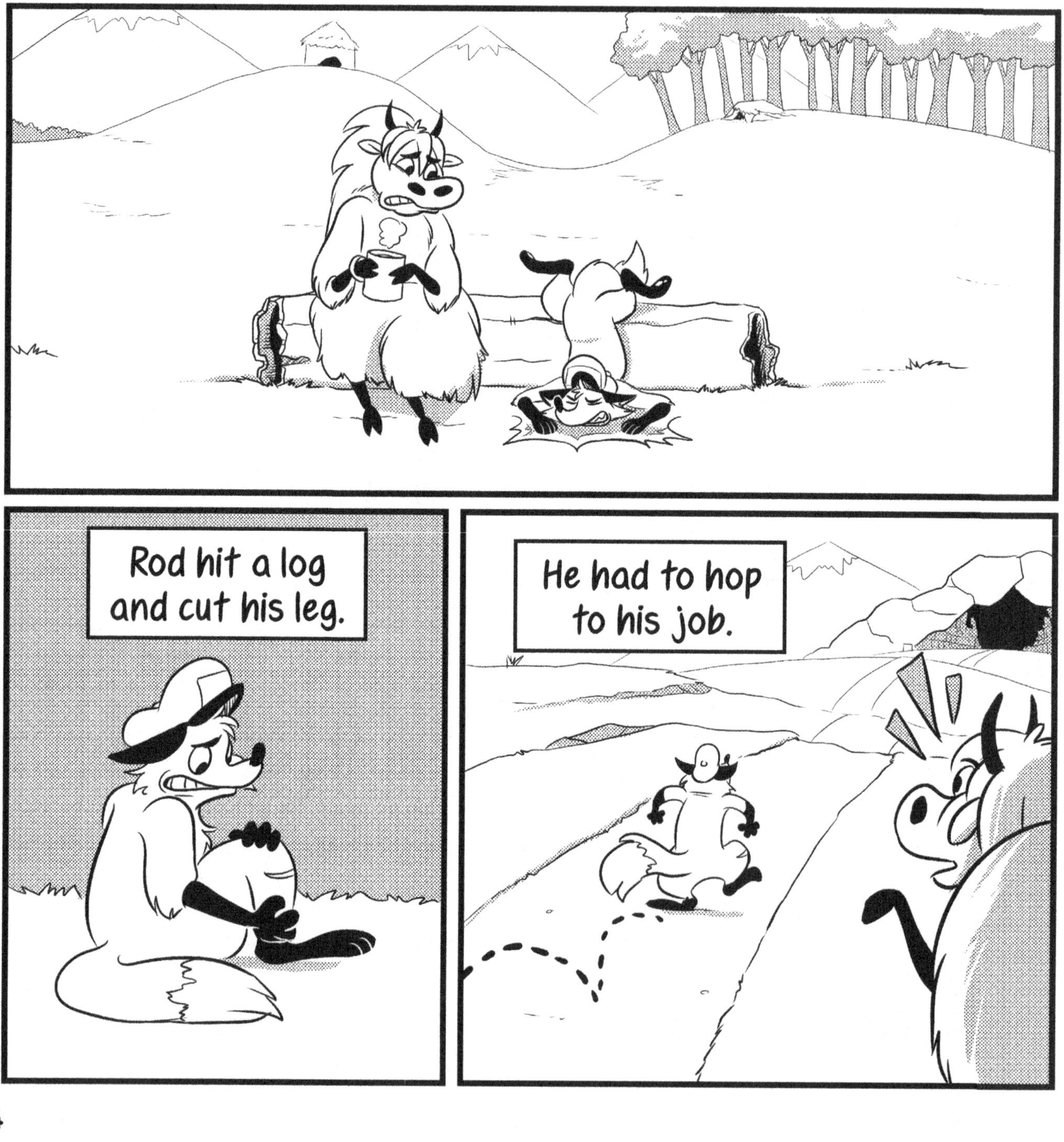
Rod hit a log
and cut his leg.
He had to hop
to his job.

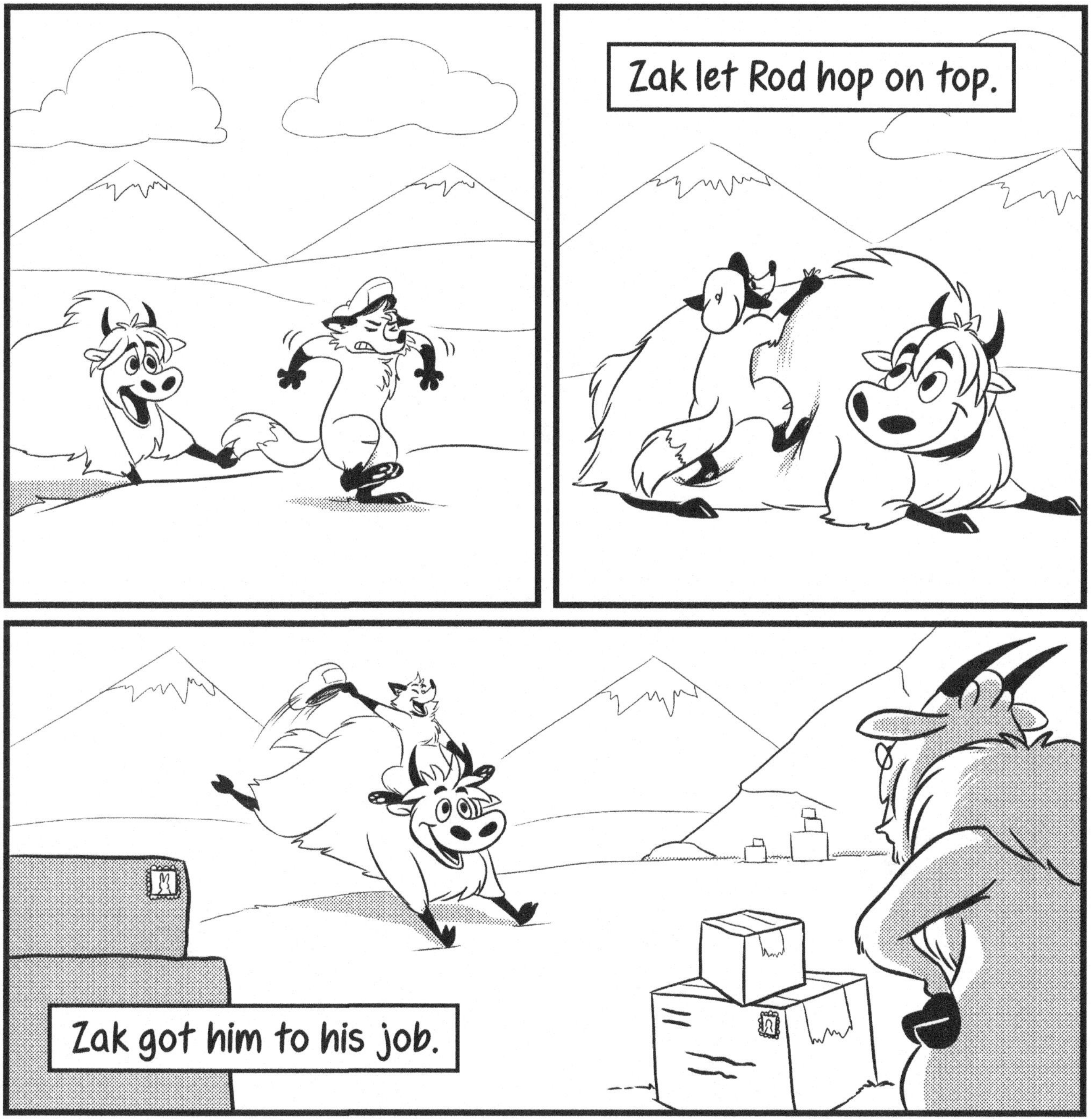
Zak let Rod hop on top.
Zak got him to his job.

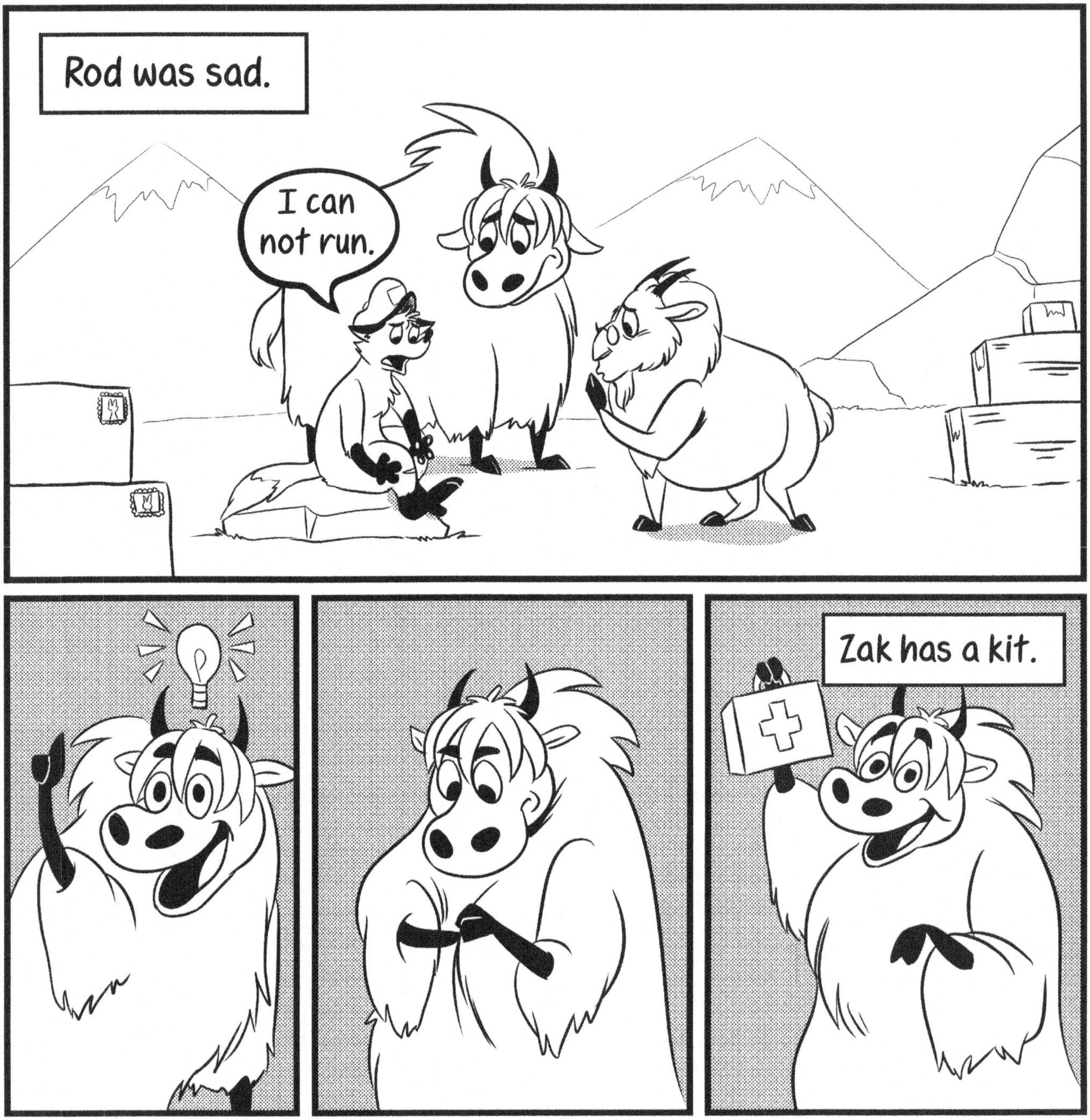
Rod was sad.
I can not run.
Zak has a kit.

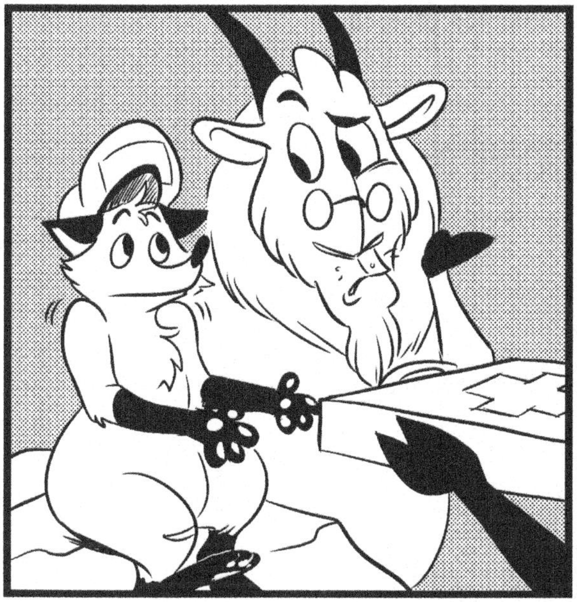

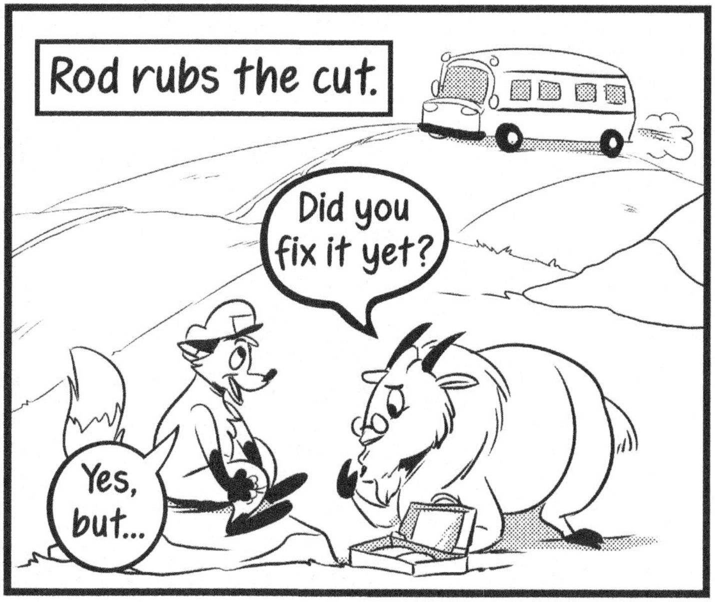
Rod rubs the cut.
Did you fix it yet?
Yes, but...

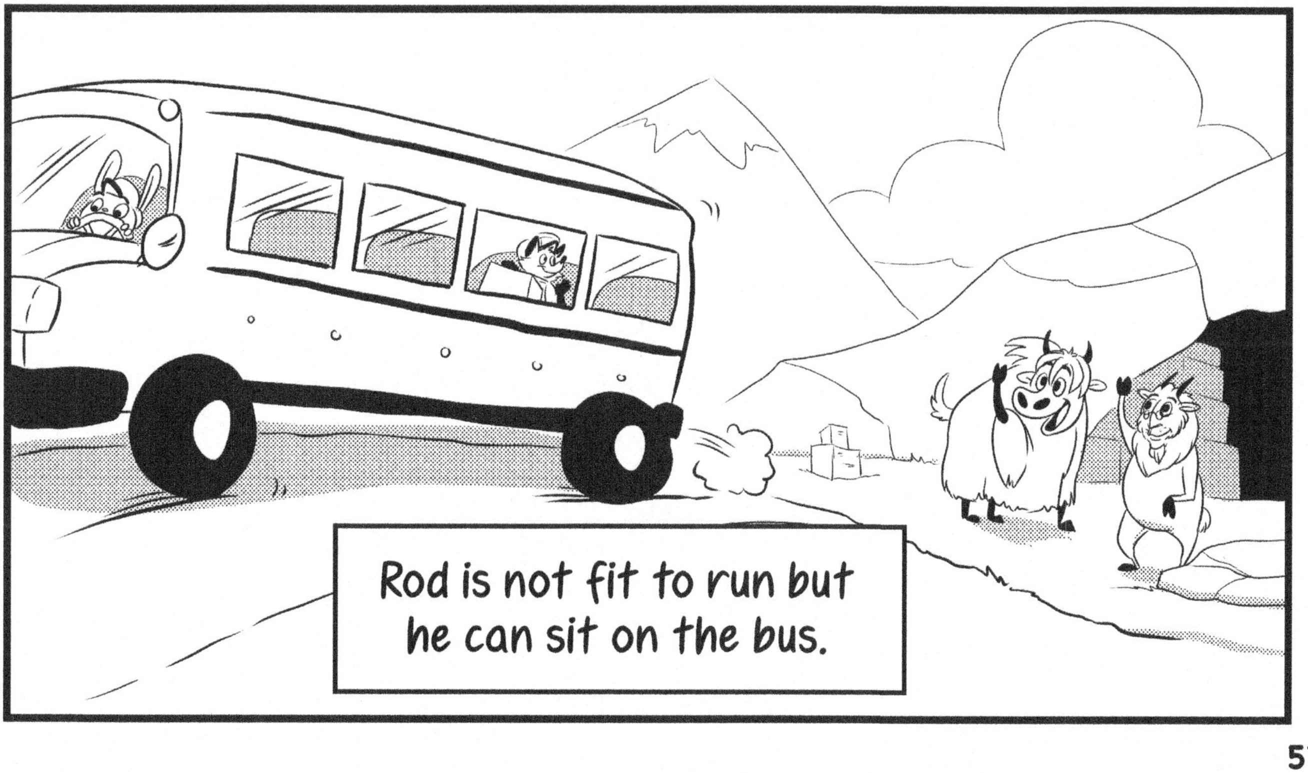
Rod is not fit to run but he can sit on the bus.

# After You Read: Rod Gets a Cut

## CHECK FOR UNDERSTANDING

1. Who lives in a hut?
2. Why was Rod sad?
3. How did Rod solve his problem?
4. Will Rod's boss be happy with Rod's solution?

## PHONOLOGICAL AWARENESS SKILLS

1. What is a word that rhymes with "*kit*"?
2. What do you get if you blend the sounds /j/ /o/ /g/?
3. How many sounds do you hear in the word "sad"?
4. Can you change the last sound in "*cut*" to /p/? What's the new word?

# CERTIFICATE OF ACHIEVEMENT!

This certificate is to show that:

can read The Yak Pack's short vowel comics!

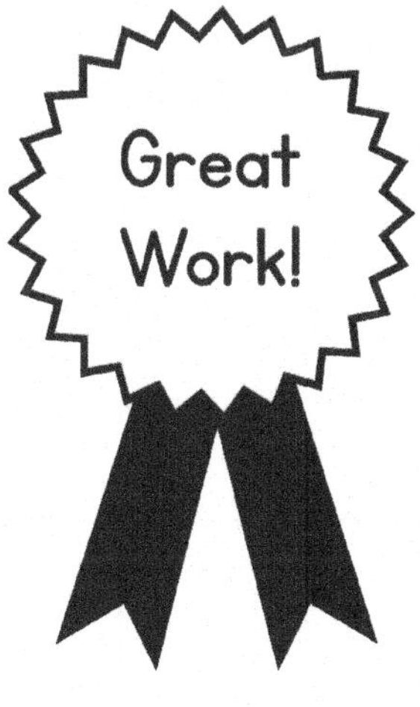
Great
Work!

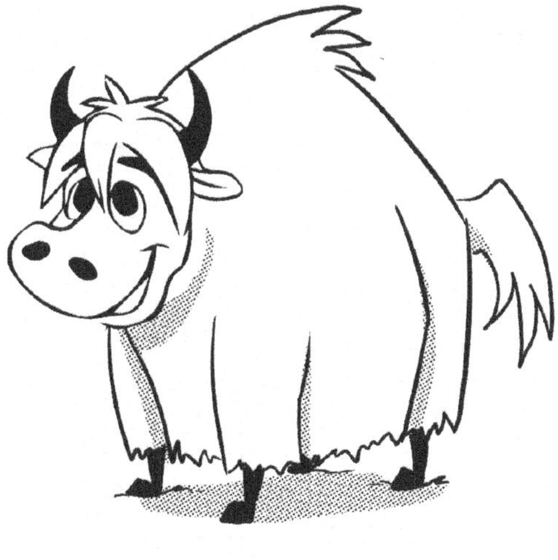

# Scope & Sequence

Collect all the Comics & Phonics from The Yak Pack!

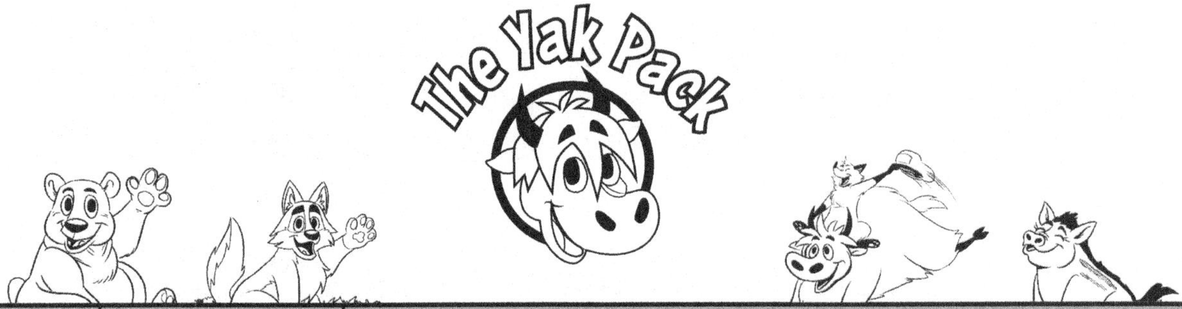
The Yak Pack

| Book | Focus | Skills Covered | |
|---|---|---|---|
| 1 | Short Vowels | Short A | Short E |
| | | Short O | Short U |
| | | Short I | Short vowel review |
| 2 | Digraphs | CH | FF, SS, ZZ, LL |
| | | SH | CK |
| | | TH | Digraph review |
| 3 | Blends | L-blends | 3-letter blends |
| | | R-blends | Digraph blends |
| | | S-blends | Blend review |
| | | Final blends | |
| 4 | Bossy E | Long A words (A_E) | Long U/E words (U_E, E_E) |
| | | Long I words (I_E) | Soft C/G Bossy E words |
| | | Long O words (O_E) | Bossy E review |

# About Rumack Resources

Rumack Resources is the publishing division of Ruth Rumack's Learning Space (RRLS), an educational support company specializing in early literacy. Since 1996, Ruth Rumack and her team have been providing individualized academic and special education support to students in Toronto, Canada. RRLS's approach to teaching through sensory and motor activities that are tailored to specific learning styles is evident in every Rumack Resources product. All products are developed and written by certified teachers with extensive experience in the early reading process.

*Author Jennifer Makwana is a certified teacher at Ruth Rumack's Learning Space. She holds a Bachelor of Education and a diploma in Early Childhood Education. Jennifer lives in Toronto with her husband and two children.*

## Titles available from Rumack Resources:

Phonological Awareness:

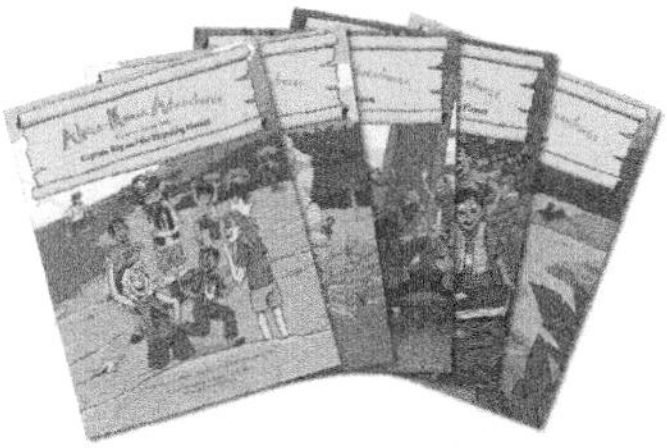

Alpha-Mania Adventures

Storybooks that teach 5 phonological awareness skills: rhyming, blending, alliteration, segmenting, and sound manipulation.

Phonics:

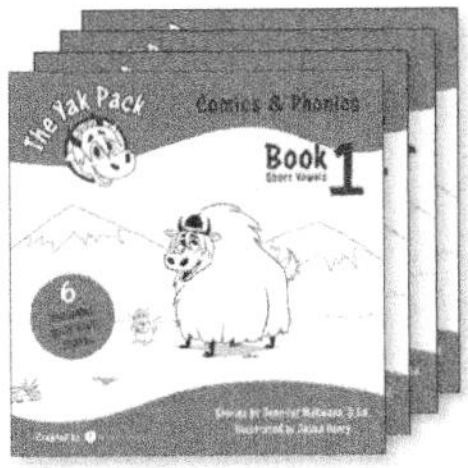
The Yak Pack
Comics & Phonics
Book 1

The Yak Pack: Comics & Phonics

Phonics readers in a fun, comic style!
Book 1: Short Vowels
Book 2: Digraphs
Book 3: Blends
Book 4: Bossy E

Sight Words:

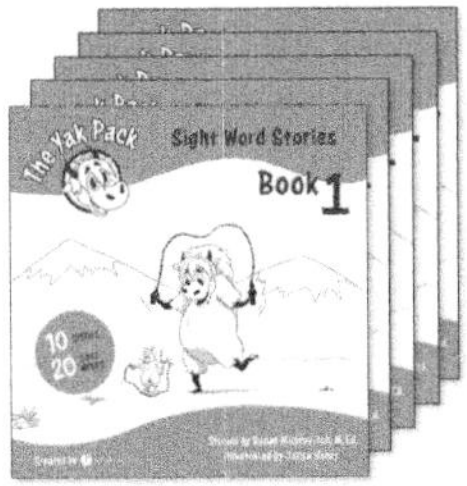
The Yak Pack
Sight Word Stories
Book 1

The Yak Pack: Sight Word Stories

Stories to teach sight words!
Book 1: Sight words 1-20
Book 2: Sight words 21-40
Book 3: Sight words 41-60
Book 4: Sight words 61-80
Book 5: Sight words 81-100

www.rumackresources.com

Made in the USA
Monee, IL
05 February 2022

90664176R00037